Blake

Lynn Thompson

Blake

PUBLISHED BY Lynn Thompson
All rights reserved
Copyright© 2010 by Lynn Thompson
Designed By: Victoria LeDuc

First Printing, April 2014
ISBN-13: 978-0-9891557-0-0

ISBN-10: 0989155706

Chapter One

"Oh Killer, it's so nice to almost be home! What a crazy last nine months. I almost forgot how beautiful the mountains are up here." I sighed as I drove the narrow road with the hairpin curves.

"Soon winter will be upon us." I grinned. "All of those brilliant gold leaves on the Aspen trees will be bare against the Pine trees, and wow, the fresh air smells fabulous." All of the tension left my body as peace from the surrounding mountains settled in. There was nobody else on the road, and as far as the eye could see were the reds, gold's, and greens of the trees.

"We're almost to Valles Calderas, wouldn't it be nice if we spot some elk herds."

Valles Calderas is a vast meadow surrounded by the mountains and is one of the largest volcanic calderas in the world. Because the meadow is so green it's hard to imagine it was once a volcano. Yellow and purple flowers dotted the grass, making it look fantastical. At one time it was private property with cows grazing on the land along with the elk, but now it's public property, empty

of the bigger wildlife until fall when the elk seem to

1

come out from hiding. That's what I was hoping for on this trip.

I've driven this road many times in my life and had different experiences each time I've come up here. Mountain lions have jumped out in front of my vehicle, racing to the other side of the forest in an awesome blur. I've seen bears, and twice I've stopped for a big herd of elk crossing the highway. A bit scary, but quite a sight. A few times I've felt like I was driving on a parallel plane. The trees and rocks seemed just a tad out of their original place. Some nights I the drive was peaceful, other nights I would get crept out on certain stretches of the road. And, of course, there were the times when the drive was surreal like now.

Once I stopped to view the vastness of the Valles Calderas and one lone coyote walked right up to my truck. We checked each other out for about ten minutes before he took off back into the valley, very cool. I love these mountains and that's why I chose to live here.

I kept my eye out for elk as Killer lay contently next to me with absolutely no interest in what was going on around him.

"Oh well, I don't see any elk this time. Too bad." We drove in silence for a while, "I have such big plans for us this winter Killer, you're going to love it up here. We're going to hike, fish, spend lots of snowy days sitting in front of the fire, and we'll have tons of peace and quiet!"

My name is Montana Dayton. I am officially on vacation. Killer's my 6-month-old, 80 pound adopted chocolate lab/ bull mastiff mix puppy. He probably doesn't

2

have a vicious bone in his body. But when he runs, which is rare, he starts foaming at the mouth. He reminds me of Stephen King's rabid Cujo. Right now he's lying in the passenger seat of my truck with his head plopped down uncomfortably on my lap.

"I have to admit I'm starting to get a little nervous." Silence from Killer.

"Okay this is something you don't know, I let Rose oversee the construction of the houses, the modeling, and the decorating of the interior. I've only seen the blueprints, so I'm not sure what we're going home to."

I adopted Killer on a whim a week ago from my mother's dog preserve in Hurley, NM. To be honest, he wouldn't stop following me around. What's a girl to do? Besides he's cute and he doesn't talk literally, I've heard a "woof" once. I can tell him all of my deep dark secrets knowing he won't tell a soul, and his greatest quality is he doesn't talk back. For the only man in my life, he's perfect.

"Okay, Killer we're almost there. See that dirt road? It leads to our casa."

I downshifted and turned on the gravel road in my big, gas guzzling Ford F-150, four wheel drive pickup, painted forest green camouflage colors. I then realized I'd made a great investment buying the truck. The ruts were horrendous and in major need of grading.

I noticed the for sale sign on the truck and fell in love. I took the beast for a test drive and purchased it right away. Besides, does it really matter that I look like a teenager driving it?

I'm 28 years old, 5'2", and the steering wheel almost touches my chin for me to reach the gas pedal. The old

3

Ford was already coming in handy. And looking younger than you really are is a good thing right?

I gazed at the landscape around me as I worked my way around the ruts. Both sides of the dirt track were thick with big beautiful Pine trees, Blue Spruces, Aspen, and some Oak bushes. The sunlight sparkled off the leaves of the trees casting a shadowy, lacy pattern over us. My truck blended in with the landscape. My skin prickled with anticipation.

I found the perfect piece of land for myself. It's a three-mile drive up the dirt road before we reach the clearing to my house. A huge meadow sits behind my back door, forest surrounds the meadow, and a big stream runs through, with good fishing from what I've been told. There's also a small wooden bridge that crosses over the stream to the other side of the forest, which is private property like mine.

"Yes, my driveway is graded!" I exclaimed as we reached the house. My driveway's shaped into a horseshoe for easy turn around access and is big enough to hold several vehicles. I pulled in, turned off the truck, and stared at the A-Frame house for a few minutes.

"This is a good sign Killer, no dragons or fairies anywhere." Killer smiled and some drool pooled out of his mouth leaving a long wet mark on my pants. I shook my head as I wiped off my leg with the bandana I'd bought just for these occasions. "Let's check out the casa, and then find Rose."

We ambled up the stairs to the front door, which is off a full deck and went inside.

"First we find the kitchen and get you some food and

4

water Killer. Killer?"

On one side of the entrance way, a long dark skinny table sat against the wall with two top drawers. Below the dresser a braided rug covered the floor, creating enough distance underneath for shoes. On the other side of the wall was a coat rack, and in the corner by the doorway was a big bunch of rosemary hanging off a silver string.

The rosemary enveloped the air with a nice pine scent. Through the entrance way is a big open space with a high ceiling and long ceiling fans hanging down. My living room sat to the right side of the entrance, and my kitchen sat to the left.

Killer was lying on the big throw rug in the living room in front of a roaring fire at Roses' feet. Rose sat in a big overstuffed chair eyeballing him.

"Is he safe?" Rose asked, scrutinizing Killer.

"Yeah, he's good."

Rose didn't seem to certain. I called Killer. He cocked his head at me, put his head on his paws and closed his eyes.

"Okay, Killer, food and water are in the kitchen when you're ready. You would think as a puppy he would want to run and play after the long drive up here."

"He doesn't look like a puppy to me." Rose examined Killer.

I laughed. "He's 6 months old; I can't wait until he grows into his gangly self." I watched him sleeping. "I'm pretty wiped out too. I want to check out the rest of the house before I hit the sack."

Rose slowly got up and tiptoed around Killer. "He's going to take some getting used to, but he does seem like a big softy. So, what do you think?" Rose asked, spreading her arms around.

"I think the house is perfect." One couch, one chair, an entertainment system with a big screen TV, stereo, two gaming systems, all the DVDs and dreaded exercise games I needed.

Rose stared at me with her eyebrows raised. "There's hardly any furniture in here. What if you decide to entertain? Where will everyone sit?"

"That's the point." I laughed. "No entertainment in my abode. Only me and Killer this winter." Don't get me wrong, I like people, just not all of the time. Besides, right now I'm on vacation.

"Let's go into the kitchen," She sighed. "You really should be more social, meet more people, find a man, and have some kids. I don't understand why you want to stay up here alone all winter.

When you get old like me you can have your "peace" time." She finger quoted peace and gave me a loving, but disappointed gaze.

"Let's not go there again. I already meet a lot of people and right now I'm on vacation. You know I don't want people to know who I am and where I live." I replied as we walked into the kitchen. "These granite counter tops and all of the new appliances are gorgeous."

I slid my fingertips over the glossy black, with dark gray specks, granite counter top. The appliances were black, and exactly what I ordered. Black is a perfect color for someone like me. I have a bad habit of spilling dark drinks and food often. The tile floor was a beautiful Santa Fe Brown with stain guard, making it super easy to clean.

"I'm proud of myself. The island I added myself to kind of separate the living room and kitchen." Rose smiled. "It sits six people; see the bar stools, six of them. Just in case you change your mind and have a few people over."

I rolled my eyes and yawned. "The kitchen is perfect Rose. What's next?"

"Solarium, then your room and bed. You can check out the rest in the morning." Rose led me to the back of the house, past the downstairs bath, and we entered the solarium. The solarium windows were made out of thick glass. The windows allowed the natural sunlight and warmth in while keeping out the cold. Rose had planted my garden in this room a few months earlier, and the plants were already bursting with fruits and vegetables.

I turned around in a full circle, admiring all of her hard work.

"Thank You, Rose. This is wonderful."

"Your room's upstairs, I'm going to go check the barn. I'll see you in the morning."

"You're an angel." I smiled and aimed for the stairs.

The spiral staircase to my left was almost dead center in the

solarium. I climbed up the wood steps, walked through my office space, longed for my bed, and went straight into the bathroom. I think it took me two minutes total to clean up, strip, and fall asleep.

The next morning I woke up to hot breath on my face and half of a dog lying on my chest. "Good morning to you too Killer," I pushed him off me. I tried to roll over to go back to sleep, but he planted his big face right in front of

7

mine. One "Woof", he sneezed. I was now covered with dog slobber.

"Thanks." I cringed as I wiped off my face with a tissue. "I suppose you want to go out?"

Killer's tail started thumping on the bed. "Okay," I yawned. "Let me get dressed. Don't make a habit out of waking me up this way."

I threw on some sweatpants and a shirt before plodding downstairs with killer on my heels. I smelled coffee as soon as I stepped into the solarium. Oh, thank you, Rose.

Taking a short detour into the kitchen, I poured some coffee. I noticed the machine was on a timer before I headed for the front door. I stepped onto the deck. The morning chill caressed my bare feet. My java steamed in the crisp air and my feet were getting cold fast. I started to say "Hurry up Killer," but he felt the same way I did. He'd already bolted inside the front door.

"My turn," I mumbled. I refilled my cup, took a long hot shower to warm up again, and applied a touch of makeup. A little blush, eyeliner, mascara, and I'm done. I stepped into my walk-in closet to rummage for some clothes and smiled. Rose had unpacked some of my boxes. I found worn jeans, a black long-sleeved, low cut, turtleneck sweater, some thick socks, black boots, and a dark green flannel shirt.

After I dressed I went back into the bathroom and contemplated my hair. It's fairly long, a tad wavy, (if I don't brush it right away) and normally reddish blond. Right now it's colored a rich dark auburn. I'd been debating on putting gold streaks in for the last week. But have been holding off out of pure laziness.

I've got a small pink rhinestone stud in my nose and a belly button ring with pink dangling rhinestones'. I'm slim, but still need to exercise. I'm the proud owner of five tattoos. Four of them are a Gaelic vine in different colors I drew myself, and one's a phoenix.

The Gaelic vines start on my left upper arm and travel up my shoulder. They snake diagonally down my back and end just past my right hip. The phoenix is on my right thigh. I had them draw the designs on me that way so I can cover them. I love tattoos.

Unfortunately, some people look down on tattoo's and think the worst. Contrary to their belief I very rarely drink and I don't do any drugs unless you count caffeine a drug. I smiled and took another hit of coffee. In my line of business, it's better to be able to cover them when I need to.

I brushed my hair and proceeded to check out my loft. My bathroom was beautifully built with granite counter tops and tiled floors in bone-gray colors. Cobalt blue streaks wound through the bone gray, adding a touch of glamor to the bathroom. The shower's built into the corner and my beloved Jacuzzi sat against the wall, both of them tiled in the same colors.

I stepped through the door and into my bedroom. My queen size, four poster bed was placed in the middle of my room. I fluffed up the cobalt blue down comforter and wandered over to my dresser. I glanced in the mirror attached to the dresser and grinned. Could life get any better than this?

I clicked on the track lighting strung across the ceiling above my bed. The cobalt blue vanity lights shined off my wood floor and radiated a soft glow onto the throw rugs.

9

Rose did an amazing job decorating. In between my bedroom and the stairs was a small office space with a desk, computer, filing cabinet, and of course some rosemary hanging from a silver string. I breathed in the scent. I still had some unpacking to do, but it could wait.

I walked downstairs, found a protein drink for breakfast, and searched for Killer. He was staring wantonly at the fireplace.

"Come on Killer, we're going to find Rose and check out the rest of the property."

He gazed longingly at the fireplace one more time before standing up and expelling a heavy sigh. I couldn't help but grin as we walked through the solarium, he was already acting spoiled. I noticed more rosemary hanging from silver string by the back door. "I wonder what that's about," I mumbled under my breath as we strolled across the deck and down the stairs.

Rose's house was built behind and to the right of mine a short distance away. A small hard packed dirt road edges off the main drive to her house, so she doesn't have to walk too far. It's built similar to mine, except her loft's the guest room, and her bedroom's where my solarium is, just a bit smaller to accommodate an extra downstairs bathroom.

I stopped abruptly halfway to her house. The hair on my arms and the back of my neck stood up on end. A creepy sensation settled over me. I glanced at Killer. He sat down, giving me his "what's up" face. I slowly turned in a circle, eying the landscape and trees surrounding me. I checked out Killer again, no reaction from him. I didn't see anything. The sensation didn't last long before everything went back to normal.

"What was that about?" I asked Killer as we started walking. I glanced at him again, not expecting him to answer and smiled. "Must be culture shock, straight from the wild city to the wild, peaceful forest." My gut told me otherwise. I ignored it. "I might need a couple of days to adjust," I said, shaking off the eeriness of the moment before.

Killer and I halted again when we reached Rose's front deck. We stared wide-eyed, taking everything in. Crystals, fairies, dragons, unicorns, and Pegasus's covered her deck. Some were in the form of statues, but most were wind catchers, sun catchers, and chimes. Pots of rosemary sat on both sides of the entranceway and one sat in front of her door.

Killer whined and planted himself below the steps.

"Okay, you stay here." I climbed the stairs up to Rose's door, announced myself and tried to enter. How weird, I thought. The door's locked. I knocked. Rose hurried out, quickly closing the door behind her.

"My house is a mess. I'll show it to you later." She huffed, almost running down the front stairs.

Rose was dressed in light teal leggings, a dark teal tie-dye long sleeve hoodie and bright red hiking boots. Her long silver hair was tied back in a braid with brilliant blue dragonfly rhinestone clips on both sides of her head, holding the wisps' of stray hair back.

Rose's full name is Rosemary Parks. I used to work for her helping out around the house. Now she works for me, kind of. The deal is she can stay on as long as she wants for free as long as she takes care of the property while I'm gone. So far everything's worked out great. She's a little

11

taller than me, but almost everyone is, a little rounder, and much older. I've never asked her age and she's never told me. I do know she acts younger than her age and looks younger too.

"I'm packing, and then I have to clean before I leave this weekend."

"Why so soon? I thought you'd be here another couple of weeks so we'd be able to spend some time together." I said pouting.

She growled. "You know my kids. They don't think I can take care of myself."

"You did tell them I would be here right?"

Another growl, "Yes, but they decided I might get stuck in a snow

storm, end up staying all winter, and break my hip from slipping on ice or something."

Rose's kids live in Los Angeles, California and desperately want her to move somewhere closer to them. Rose can't stand the smog or the noise pollution, so she visits for a couple of months once a year over the holidays to pacify them.

"Anyhow," she said as we started walking to the barn with Killer on our heels, "I had the solar panels rechecked, they're good to go, and the wood pile's full thanks to Bear."

"Who's Bear? And what's with the hanging rosemary in my house?"

She got this huge grin on her face "You'll meet Bear later today. He's invited us to an early dinner. The rosemary's for protection against evil spirits, negative energy, and to prevent illness. I read about it in a book.

12

You should burn some every once in a while too."

I pondered that for a minute. No evil spirits were allowed on my land or in my house. I hardly ever got sick and negative energy was definitely not allowed on this trip. I could handle the rosemary, I'd just add it to the growing list of Rose's little quirks. Bear, on the other hand, would hopefully be Roses age.

Rose stalled at the barn door, turned around and peered at me like she was trying to read my mood. "How did you sleep last night?"

"Really good. What's up, Rose? Is there a problem? You've been acting weird all morning."

"Well, we adopted a barn cat," she tossed her braid back while eyeballing Killer, "her name is Pumpkin."

I side stepped her and entered the barn. On the right, shelves reached close to the ceiling. Most of them full of odds and ends for my horse. A plank leaned against the side for a catwalk. On the top shelf was a huge orange tabby cat with yellow eyes.

"She keeps the mice away," Rose said.

"I bet."

Pumpkin looked like she had her fill of mice, along with the dried cat food on the top shelf. The cat had to weigh 20 plus pounds. There was no telling where the hair ended and the fat began.

Rose's back came up. "I found her in town. No one would claim her, so here she is."

"It's okay Rose" I mumbled as the cat began to hiss at us. "I'm sure we could use a barn cat."

Pumpkin hissed again louder, apparently she'd noticed Killer. Killer sat down and whined at Pumpkin. Pumpkin

13

glared down at him.

"I'm going to finish checking out the barn and say hi to Lightning." I walked into the stall with Rose right on my heels.

"There's something else I need to tell you." Her voice sounded rushed.

I have four stalls in my barn and one horse. I found two.

"You took up horseback riding?"

"No," She replied from right behind me. "You know I only like horses from a distance. I meant to talk to you, but I've been busy. That horse there is Ace and he belongs to Max."

"Who's Max?"

"Oh, you'll like him. I offered him use of the barn in exchange for Chase." Rose grinned.

"Who's Chase?" I asked, wondering if Rose was being vague on purpose.

Rose sighed, "He's the kid taking care of the horses. Max is paying him to come take care of Ace and Lightning while he builds his barn. Plus Chase said he'd take care of Pumpkin for me too. Chase likes Pumpkin."

"Why does this guy Max own a horse and no barn?"

"He's got wolves," She replied like I should already be aware of this. "Look I'm not comfortable with you staying here alone all winter."

"So you're bringing people into my vacation I don't know!" I was starting to growl now. "Rose I have a video cam on my computer to talk to my family, Killer, Lightning, now Pumpkin, and a truck. I won't be isolated up here."

14

"You'll like Max and Chase," she humphed, putting her foot down. "Subject closed!" She stomped out of the barn.

I blew out a breath and rubbed Aces nose. Ace gave me the impression he was a top breed horse, but I don't know much about horses. He stood tall with a mix of gray and white hair, white mane and tail. Gorgeous.

I frowned, my first day here and already I was becoming stressed. I closed my eyes, rolled my shoulders and relaxed by picturing his owner as a short, pudgy, balding, middle-aged man, who needed wolves, and a gorgeous horse to feed his ego. I smiled and held onto the image.

Lightning's my horse. She's in the stall across from Ace. She's a sleek black female with four white socks, black mane, and a black tail. I think she's a mutt. She doesn't carry the same princely demeanor as Ace. I adopted her down in Hurley because I wanted a sweet horse to ride up here. I grabbed a brush, stepped into her stall, and started brushing her, wondering again what had come over Rose.

"Woof!" I snapped out of my zone, put away the brush, and went to make sure Killer wasn't killing Pumpkin. Nope, he still had his eye's glued to her, but now his tail thumped on the hay-strewn floor. I glanced up at the cat. Not too upset. Good.

"Come on Killer, I suppose we should get ready to meet Bear."

Chapter Two

Rose stood on the deck waiting for us when we reached the house.

"Hi Rose," I said, keeping an eye on her mood. "Hope you weren't waiting too long."

"Nope, I just got here."

"Good, let me grab my purse and we'll head out." I jogged into the house and returned in a flash.

"What did you tell Bear about me?"

"Only that you've had great luck as an investor. I'm taking my own vehicle down so I can visit with him longer. You can follow me."

"Okay," I said as we all piled into my Ford.

I dropped Rose off at her rundown blue jeep. Anyone who knew Rose could see her coming from a mile away. The tailgate of her jeep was covered with stickers of fairies frolicking in the woods and she had a small crystal unicorn with a gold horn and hoofs hanging from her rear-view mirror. She pulled onto the dirt road and we carefully maneuvered around the deep ruts toward the paved road.

Within ten minutes we reached the small town Killer and I had passed through the day before. The town consisted of the basics for mountain life, an automotive garage with towing and snow plows, a bed and breakfast, a place that sells fishing supplies along with horse rentals and snowmobiles, a gas station that also sells some winter apparel, and, of course, a bar and grill. We pulled into the parking lot of Pops Bar and Grill and got out of our vehicles.

"Does Bear own this place?" I asked as my eyes gazed over the exterior of the bar.

"Yep, it's been in his family for a long time."

We climbed the steps up to the rectangular building and on to a narrow deck. The only window on this side of the building was on the front door. The sign in the window said closed.

"It's not open Rose."

"Not open to the general public right now. Bear put this together special for us before business hours. He wanted to have some extra free time to meet you. We'll go around back."

We rounded the side of the building and stepped onto a full deck in the back with high railings. Well-placed solid wood picnic tables covered most of the open area. The stunning view from the back deck caught my eye.

The deck stood, at least, five feet off the ground. A few feet beyond was the same stream by my house, but wider, making it a river. On the other side of the river, a rock bed sloped up to the tree line with purple mountains set against the crisp blue sky.

While I was enjoying the view Bear must have come out of the bar, because I heard Rose croon.

I turned around. My first thought was thank goodness

17

this wasn't a find Montana a man set up. My second thought was, now I understand why everyone calls him Bear.

Bear's a big guy with more muscle than fat. His demeanor screamed rugged mountain man. At first glance, he seemed to be about the same age as Rose, whatever that is, but then I realized he's probably a bit older. He has shoulder length sandy blond hair, mixed with gray. His beard and mustache were solid gray and his sharp blue eyes were surrounded by laugh lines. He looked like a big bear, but not as hairy. He also adored Rose.

I sat down at one of the picnic tables and waited for them to stop goggle-eying each other. Watching them was both endearing and embarrassing. Endearing because they were kind of old, embarrassing for the same reason.

Bear pulled his eyes away from Rose and noticed me sitting at the table. He interlocked his hand with hers and came over to introduce himself.

"Hi, I'm Tom Tomson," he said. "You must be Montana."

"Very nice to meet you," Tom Tomson I thought, no wonder he liked being called Bear.

"The pleasure's all mine," he said smiling, "but call me Bear. I hardly ever answer to Tom."

"Okay Bear" My eyes wandered back to the mountains. "This is a wonderful place you have. The view is absolutely enchanting and the landscape looks like an oil painting."

"Thank you," he glanced at the mountains with a grin. "It's the reason I moved up here. Follow me and I'll give you the grand tour. Afterward, you ladies can help me set

18

up for the feast."

I didn't want to move from my seat. Nature's energy seemed to flow through me, wrapping her lovely hands around me. I could sit on the deck forever with the sun beating warmly down on me.

I took another moment to enjoy the surrealism of the day before entering the bar and grill. I found the interior bigger than I'd imagined. A stage for bands and a dance floor faced the left side of the room. The tall wood tables and chairs were strategically placed along the edge of the dance floor to the center of the restaurant. A good size walkway lay in between the tables and the bar. The bar covered most of the wall. A long mirror was bolted up behind the shelves of glasses and bottles of alcohol. Bar stools sat in a neat row, waiting for costumers to come in and claim them. The kitchen was located behind the bar to the right through some double doors.

I wandered around and scanned the pictures on the walls while Rose and Bear disappeared into the kitchen. Most of the pictures consisted of a hunter bagging his animal, or a fisherman catching his fish. A few pictures, I assumed, were a younger Bear and his family. When the pictures had circled me back to the bar I started collecting the items they'd put out for our feast. I took them outside and placed them on the picnic table closest to the river. Bear and Rose joined me. We all sat down and dove in. We were starving.

"Ooh, what is the meat? It's so good!" I asked Bear.

"That's smoked elk. I shot a big one this year." He said smiling.

I loaded my plate with smoked elk, potato salad, corn

on the cob, and rolls. While I ate I debated on how many pieces of peach cobbler I wanted. And how long it would take me to burn off all of the calories I had already consumed.

Once we were done eating and rearranging our jeans so we could plow into the peach cobbler Bear glanced up at me from his plate, "I have an ulterior motive for feeding you."

"Really? What's that?" My eyes drifted to the cobbler.

"Rose says you're an investor and I wanted to talk to you about investing in my business."

"Is your business doing badly?"

"No, but me and my son want to add on, were thinking about having a few people invest with us."

"Hmm…," my first real day of vacation and already someone wanted to discuss business.

Bear's grin widened "I actually don't want to go into detail now. I need to open the bar and I know you're on vacation, but I'd like to meet with you later. Maybe in a week or two with my son if that's alright with you?"

"It's perfect. It gives me a little time to settle in." I sighed with relief, under my breath.

"Well," Bear said as he stood up "I have to go to work now."

"The food was fabulous," both Rose and I announced together.

"I'll help you pick up, then Killer and I are going home to for the night."

"You're more than welcome to stay for a drink." Bear said looking at Rose, but speaking to me.

"I brought my own car down, I'll be staying," Rose

20

replied, blushing.

"I still need to unpack, but thank you." I grinned.

"Well, come inside anyway, I have a few elk steaks for you and steak bones for Killer, your horribly vicious looking attack dog," Bear said laughing.

I started laughing too. Killer hung his head down a notch. I swear his fur turned a blush color as he followed us through the door.

We finished cleaning up then Bear hefted a heavy cooler full of meat and bones into the truck. We all said goodbye and I headed for home. All I could think about was changing into sweats and starting a fire.

My senses pricked as soon as I pulled into my driveway. I was being watched. The hair on the back of my neck and arms stood to attention and a chill crawled up my spine.

I examined the area, nothing seemed out of place, but that didn't matter. The forest surrounded me, shadows danced as the cool breeze ebbed and flowed through the trees. If something was hidden in the woods watching me it could be hiding behind one of the huge pines, or oak bushes, or anywhere.

I parked and slightly turned my head to glance at Killer. He must be a defect. He wasn't reacting at all to the unseen vibes floating off the wind. I thought animal's had a sixth sense about stuff like this and Rose never mentioned being spooked. My nerves shook, panic tried to take over my clear thinking. I inhaled several deep breaths to calm myself and glanced around again. Knowing my doors were unlocked made me feel a little better. I wouldn't have to mess around with a key, but at the same time, someone might have been in my house or might still be.

"Okay, Killer we're getting out, grabbing the meat and running for the door. This is important so you'd better be listening. If anything moves out there I want you to attack. Got it Killer?"

He yawned. I think he was ignoring me, but at least, he was ready to get out of the truck. I searched for anything I could use for a weapon. I found absolutely nothing so I threw open the door before I lost my nerve.

"Come on Killer!" I whispered as I hauled out the cooler and booked it up to the deck. I flew into the house with Killer on my heels, slammed and locked the door behind me then raced to the back locking that door too. After sliding down onto the floor and collecting my nerves, I realized the spooky sensation had dissipated.

"Ugh, what the hell is wrong with me?" I shook my head. "Nothing, I'll figure this out."

As my jitters subsided I walked back into the living room to check on Killer. He stood gazing at the fireplace with such longing I had to start a fire for us or feel guilty for thinking of my own needs first. Once the logs started to burn he settled down on the floor and closed his eyes. I put the meat away and bolted upstairs, time to start unpacking and get on the computer.

I found my smokes in the first box I unpacked and lit one. My 357 Revolver showed up in the fifth box, with the bullets. I loaded bullets into the gun and searched my house, rechecking the doors. Whoever was watching me hadn't been in the house, at least not that I could tell. I changed into my sweats and fluffy pink socks before kicking back on the couch with my laptop. I thought about calling Rose and telling her, but she would have said something to me if she was having problems. I also had to take into consideration my ability to pick up on strange occurrences and some paranormal activities along with sensing other people and their intentions.

Not saying these episodes were in anyway paranormal. A mad psycho serial killer might be on the loose, on my land.

I spent the rest of the night on the computer, researching escaped convicts and haunted lands, coming up with nothing. I wasn't any closer to finding out what may be on my property. I set down my computer and fell asleep on my couch, thinking The next morning I woke up so stiff I could barely move.

Mental note, buy a bigger couch or make it to my bed.

I stood up, did some yoga stretches, found my gun, made some coffee, and reached the front door with Killer by my side. I hid my gun in my coat pocket and headed for Rose's house. Her jeep wasn't in the driveway and she didn't answer her door. She probably spent the night with Bear, good for her.

After showering, more coffee and making sure, we had everything we needed for winter I had time to do some scouting around the property and maybe go fishing. I put on my favorite black hiking boots, black leather trench coat, and slid my gun into the back waist of my jeans. I'm not overly fond of guns but I know how to shoot and can hit whatever I need to.

On the way out the door, I picked up my fishing

23

supplies and my camera.

"Come on Killer, we're going out." He yawned big and gave me his "you're crazy" look before ambling out the door.

Rose's jeep sat in her driveway when we passed her house. Since I didn't feel up to talking to her anymore we went straight to the barn and surprised Pumpkin. The poor cat didn't have a chance to take two steps before Killer pounced, putting one huge paw on her. She rolled onto her back, attempting to play dead while he sniffed her everywhere before starting to give her a bath. I laughed and watched them for a minute. I was pretty sure the cat wanted to die out of humiliation and the "please help me" glare on her face was priceless.

I left Pumpkin to fend for herself and wandered to the stalls, wondering briefly when I would meet Max and Chase. I rubbed Aces nose. I love Lightning, but she's a poke like Killer. Ace's stance showed the power he carried in the muscles of his legs. I'd bet he could run fast, and I might need a fast horse while I scouted the woods. I weighed the consequences of borrowing Ace before deciding I'd take my chances with Lightning.

With Lightning saddled up, I called Killer. He took his paw off Pumpkin and left her drenched in his dog slobber.

"At least, you didn't get swallowed whole," I told her, laughing again. The cat gave me the evil eye and bounded up to her shelf.

We spent two hours making a loop around my property, looking for any kind of evidence a lunatic resided on my land and came up empty handed. I hadn't been spooked since last night, so we decided to stop at the stream and go fishing. While we were kicking it, waiting for the fish to bite, I secretly hoped they wouldn't, because Yuk, I hated gutting fish, I thought about the property next to mine. We'd passed the bridge to my neighbor's a short way back and I decided I wanted to cross the river and scout that area in the morning.

Either I was losing my mind or something planted itself on my land. I was rooting for the later.

My eyelids drifted closed. The warmth of the sun beat down on my face and I began to relax. Within a few short minutes, the awareness of eyes on me pin-pricked my senses. I glanced around with my lids still at half mast, slowly I put down my pole, took a deep breath and concentrated on which direction the vigilant energy was coming from. I jumped up and turned in the direction of the bridge in one fluid movement with my gun drawn.

A drop dead gorgeous guy sat on top of Ace grinning at me. My blood began to boil with just the thought of him spying on me. I stepped forward, ready to march right up to him and give him a piece of my mind when I caught something in my peripheral vision flashing through the bushes. My heart stopped beating for a second, tingling assaulted my skin, causing every strand of hair on my arms to rise. I spun around and slowly turned in a circle with my gun drawn. There was nothing there. I returned my attention to the horse and rider, most likely Max. He had disappeared too. Dropping my arms, I heaved a sigh. Something was definitely haunting me, I just needed to figure out what.

I packed up and hopped onto Lightning's back. I placed my gun in my pocket for easier excess and trotted

25

Lightning back to my place, keeping my eyes open for anything and everything that moved around me.

When we reached the barn I unloaded Lightning's saddle and harness, brushed her down, fed her and hiked up to Rose's house. I left Killer at the stairs, he still wasn't brave enough to pass through all of the do-dads on her deck. I banged on her door. The door swung open as Rose stepped out.

"Hi," Rose said, a little bit surprised I stood on her front porch, "let's sit in the chairs around back. It's gonna be cold real soon, so we might as well enjoy these last few days of warmth."

We sat down, enjoying the view for a few minutes. This was another reason I moved up here. The sun sat low in the sky creating an incredible sunset of pastel pinks and lavender colors. Soon the stars would be out and up here in mountains the universe seemed close enough to touch.

I took a second to scan the landscape for anything out of the ordinary.

"What's up?" asked Rose. "You're starting to creep me out."

Great! I'm starting to creep Rose out and there's something out there more threatening. Go figure.

"I need more information on Max. What does he look like? What does he do?"

Rose laughed. "Did you finally meet him?"

"Maybe," in a roundabout way, I thought to myself.

"Well, he's a handsome young man, probably a few years older than you and he's very nice."

"And?"

"And what?"

26

"Describe him for me please."

Rose sighed, "Max is tall, dark and handsome. He's got black hair and intense gray eyes."

"Anything else?"

She blushed, "I wasn't really checking him out you know. I kinda got a man."

I smiled. "I thought you might have something with Bear. What does Max do?"

"Yeah," Rose said all dreamy eyed, "I really like Bear." She glanced at me. "Max said he worked for the government, but that's all. Any more questions I have a date tonight."

"One more then I'll let you go. Have you noticed anything strange happening around here?"

"No, everything's fine. Are you all right?"

I smiled, glad Rose wasn't bothered by the weirdness that was throwing me off kilter.

"Yeah, probably just culture shock. Do me a favor Rose and be careful if you're coming in at night. There are bears, coyotes, mountain lions, and all kinds of wild animals up here."

"Don't worry about me," she laughed, "and don't forget about Max's wolves. His wolves might be what's making you nervous."

I'd forgotten about the wolves, besides my gut told me animals weren't the problem. And I didn't think Max was the watcher I felt either. I exhaled a deep breath. I would figure out who was watching me. I had to be patient.

"Have fun tonight," I said standing up.

Rose blushed again. "I will." She hurried back inside.

I went home, started a fire, and rummaged in the

27

cabinet for some Oreo cookies.

"I'm getting in the bath," I told Killer as I checked my doors to make sure they stayed secure. I carried my gun, cookies, and some water, I don't like milk much, up to the bathroom and settled into relax mode. I left the tub looking like a prune, put my robe on and found some warm fluffy socks. Time to get down to business, I grabbed my laptop and went back downstairs. I hoped to find some geographical maps of my property and my neighbor's.

I didn't get far. As a matter of fact, I stretched out on the couch, turned on the TV, and lights out Montana.

When I woke up stiff again I started thinking about bringing my bed downstairs, I mean what's the use of having a one if I didn't even sleep in it. I stretched, worked out some of the kinks in my muscles and smelled coffee. At once I opened my eyes and reached for my gun, which, of course, sat on the counter in the bathroom. Probably a good thing I thought, I'm sure it's just Rose, after all, she's the only one with the extra key to my house. But I didn't sense Rose. I threw my legs over the couch and limped toward the kitchen. That's when I wished I had my gun.

This is ridiculous, I thought as I glared at Killer and poured myself some coffee. Max sat comfortably at my table, smiling at me, looking hot, and drinking my coffee. If I'd had my gun on me I'm sure the threat of seeing it would have forced him out of my house quicker.

"I was going to make you breakfast, but I didn't find any eggs or bacon in your refrigerator, only protein drinks."

"You must be Max. How did you get in?"

"Trade secret," he held out his hand for me to shake,

28

"and you must be Montana."

I glanced at his hand, glared at Killer again, and sat down across from him.

Killer wagged his tail and grinned as if to say "everything's good."

"What do you want?" I said, trying to glare at Mr. tall, dark and handsome.

I'm not sure the glare had the effect I wanted it to have. My blood rushed to my ears and my heart tried to leap out of my chest. My reaction to his sexiness set me on edge and to top it off I sat at the table in only my robe and my socks.

Max was one of those guys you admire from a distance. The hot boy next door, the one who's friendly, but already taken. I've known a few in my lifetime.

His shoulder length black hair lit up with a blue tint when the rays of sun peeked through the window. I wanted to brush my fingers through his hair.

I chuckled under my breath, I needed to brush my fingers through my own hair and wash my face. I didn't want to imagine what I looked like this morning, after sleeping on the couch.

I watched as his lean muscles flex under his clothes with the slightest of movements. My stomach tightened a notch. I gazed into his steel gray eyes and became entranced with the blue specks in them. He's taller than me, at least, 5'9 or more, I couldn't tell, because we were sitting down, and he's a couple year's older than me. I sat back in my chair as far as I could. I'd have to keep at least a ten-foot distance from him, if not more.

"I wanted to introduce myself over breakfast."

"I don't eat breakfast. Are you married?" I couldn't believe that just came out of my mouth.

"No."

"Do you have a girlfriend?" Damn, I did it again.

Max's smile grew "No."

I stood up pointing to the door. "Get out."

Max stood up, still smiling, and raised an eyebrow. "I'll go, but I'm coming back in a few hours. We'll meet for lunch. That will give you enough time to wake up and get dressed."

I gazed up at him. Max was taller than I originally thought, somewhere around 6'1 or 6'2. He towered over me.

Max gave Killer a scratch behind the ears, squatted down face to face with him and told him he was a good boy.

"What's your dog's name?"

"Killer."

He laughed, "I love it."

I locked the door behind him, went upstairs, put on some sweats, and grabbed my gun. A good workout was in order, guys like him; especially single made me nervous. They knew they were hot and used it to their advantage. I found a DVD with a lot of punching and kicking and proceeded to get rid of some of my anger. No way was I going to meet him for lunch or anything else. I pictured a moth being drawn to a flame, saw me as the moth, and started punching harder.

I finished my workout exhausted and sore. I wanted a nap but had to shower and leave before Max returned. Maybe he would get the hint and stay away if I wasn't home.

I threw on my clothes and makeup in no time. I never got the chance to get my map, so I would have to wing the scouting trip. I lit a cigarette and peeked in my fridge. Hmm… protein drinks, I took out two along with a bottle of water before searching my cabinets for food, trail mix, granola bars, and Oreos. I ate an Oreo while stuffing more in a bag with some trail mix, and a couple of granola bars. I needed to go shopping

"Come on Fluffy," I said to Killer, he whimpered. I still held on to some anger at him for letting Max in. "If I didn't love you I'd consider trading you in for a real guard dog." I glanced at him again and laughed. "Stop pouting, it's not going to work."

I marched down to the barn with Killer still sulking beside me.

"You stay here Killer, I'll be right out, besides I'm sure Pumpkin has a big enough complex from yesterday."

Ace's stall stood empty, so I quickly saddled Lightning, led her out of the barn, and ran right into Max. I cursed under my breath. He sat tall on Ace and they both looked magnificent. Ace with his sleek white hair glistening in the sun and Max with his black hair, sunglasses, and black leather jacket contrasted perfectly. Max's blue jeans hugged his legs just enough to show his well-defined muscles. I quickly mounted Lightning. Once I obtained a better eye level with Max I tried to figure out what to do.

"Nice day for a ride." he said grinning.

"I figured I'd have enough time to exercise Lightning before lunch." Liar. I hated lying, but I also felt the need to

31

be nice to Max.

"You weren't planning on meeting me for lunch, so what are you plans?"

"You can't prove that. I think we should cancel anyway, I'd like to check out my property and enjoy the weather before it snows."

"I'll join you."

He was enjoying this way too much, he was smiling way too much, and I was starting to get crankier. I suddenly felt like I was a magnet for strays.

"I'm sure you have better things to do than follow me around."

"Nope, nothing I can think of." His Cheshire cat grin showed his perfect white teeth.

Chapter Three

We rode in silence, thinking our own thoughts when Max suddenly stopped at the same place I'd been yesterday when I saw him. The bridge remained upstream, where I wanted to be.

"Why did we stop?"

"To take a break, the animals need some water."

"Okay." I dismounted, grabbed a protein drink, granola bar, and the trail mix. My stomach growled loudly at the mere sight of food. A light blush crept up my cheeks at the sound.

"There's more, help yourself," I told Max as I stretched, bit the granola bar in half and chugged the protein drink to quiet my hunger.

He laughed. "Here's my proof you weren't going to meet me for lunch."

I gave him my most innocent look. "It's a snack."

He chuckled. "It appears we're having lunch together after all."

Oh, brother. We ate in silence. When we finished off the last of the trail mix we mounted up and rode to the edge of my property.

33

"Spill it, Max, what do you want?"

"To enjoy your company."

I stopped. "I don't believe you, what do you really want?"

"I really am enjoying your company. Let's go."

"I'm not moving, but you can leave."

"I don't want to do this here," He said as he surveyed our surroundings. "We'll go back to your place and talk."

I stared deep into his eyes for a moment. He knew what was going on. The problem was, I didn't think he wanted to tell me.

I followed him back to the barn, we unsaddled the horses, brush them down, and tossed them some hay without saying a word to each other. I wanted to hear him out, but I needed to be mentally prepared for what he had to tell me also. I mean, what was so important that he couldn't tell me on the horse ride? I caught myself, maybe I was overreacting and he did just want to spend time with me. We headed up to my place. I started coffee brewing while Max stoked the fire.

"Coffee's done. I'm sure you can find everything you need." I left him to pour his own coffee and took my smokes out of my coat pocket. I found an ashtray and sat down in the chair by the fire keeping some distance between us.

"I take my coffee black," Max glowered as he sat on the couch across from me and gazed into my eyes "I know everything about you, Montana. I've decided you need to be protected."

Talking about getting straight to the point.

"Excuse me, I don't need a protector. What do you

34

know about me?"

Max held my gaze. "You and your sister won the lottery, that's why you're living up here."

"I'm living up here because I love the mountains," which was also true, plus I didn't want people constantly on my doorstep.

"And because no one up here has any inkling you're worth a ton of money," he put his hand up to keep me from speaking. "You're also a sensitive, you pick up on things not many other people do. It's what makes you so good at investing in small businesses. You have the intuition, who will succeed and who will fail."

"Everybody has that ability." He'd done his homework. I wasn't thrilled he'd dug this deep into my past.

"That ability comes naturally to you." He almost snarled, my attitude frayed his nerves.

"So, why do I need a protector?"

"You know why," he said grimly.

"No I don't, please explain your reasons to me." I needed to know what I was up against.

Rose rapped on the door. Figures, I thought as I stashed my smokes under the chair and yelled: "Come in." Rose didn't know I smoked and I wasn't in the mood for a lecture.

"Wow," She said bustling through the door straight to the fireplace. "It got real cold outside real quick. Max what a pleasant surprise."

Bear stomped in right behind her. "I brought steaks for the grill."

"I'll give you a hand," Max said to Bear as his eyes

traced over my face. He stood up, "I could use a refill on my coffee."

Great! I was still in the dark about what was going on. I had a split second vision of kicking Rose and Bear out on their butts and cornering Max for some answers. Instead, I watched Max follow Bear out of the room and gave myself an inward mental shake. I should stick with figuring this out on my own. I didn't need or want Max in my life anyway.

While the men tended to dinner in the kitchen Rose turned to me, "I need to talk to you after they leave tonight."

"Okay, when are you leaving for Cali?"

"Two days and Bear would like to spend the day with me tomorrow, so we'll talk tonight."

"Do you mind if I drive you to the airport? I have some errands to run."

Rose laughed, "I hoped you would, Bear has a big party he's throwing for a customer that day, and I would prefer not to leave my car at the airport for the next couple of months." Her frown turned into a sighed, "I would rather stay here this winter, but my family would pack up and move in with me if I did, neither of us wants that." She grinned again. "The boys are heading out to grill. I'm gonna see if they need help."

My eyes followed Rose, Bear and Max as they stepped outside onto the deck. As soon as the door closed behind them I raced upstairs and stashed my gun under my pillow.

Everyone appeared perfectly comfortable talking and cooking around the grill. I sat down on the back stairs for a little me time before dinner. The sun had set, darkness covered the peaks of the trees even though the stars lit up the sky. The night was ghostly quiet, not one creature stirred. The whole scene set an eerie landscape around me. I almost didn't feel like I sat on the same planet as everyone else.

"Nice evening," Bear said, startling me out of my reverie.

"Yes, it is," I replied as he sat down next to me.

"Thank you for taking Rose to the airport for me."

"Not a problem."

"I have a special day planned for her tomorrow, so I'll be picking her up early in the morning." Bear grinned before becoming serious. "I'll be taking Max home tonight per Roses request."

"Thanks."

Bear shifted on the stairs, glanced back to make sure Rose and Max were busy, then leaned into me, "I understand you just met me and may not want my advice, but be careful of Max. He's not an open person and no-one around here knows him very well."

"I'm already doing that, I promise." I stood up, "they're taking the steaks in."

Bear was right, I didn't know him well enough to trust his advice and I didn't know Max well enough to trust him either. I could only trust my instincts on both of their intentions. Bear didn't seem to have any bad intentions, Max I wasn't sure of.

Everyone sat down at the island Rose added for entertaining. The steaks melted like butter in your mouth and somehow baked potatoes and salads were added to the menu. I hadn't even noticed those being whipped up, but the meal ended up being exactly what I needed.

Dinner was an amazingly quiet event. Rose sat next to me and Bear sat next to Max. Bear and Rose seemed happy watching each other. I caught Max staring at me a few times. Killer sat at the end of the table waiting patiently for leftovers, and because of his good behavior, he was rewarded with some steak bones. Killer took them to the fireplace to gnaw on them while we cleaned up and somehow, afterward, Bear got Max to the door and out of the house.

"I'll walk you home Rose," I said wishing I hadn't put away my gun. Rose seemed to be in a hurry after everyone left and I didn't want to keep her any longer.

I called to Killer, he glanced at me, picked up a bone and made himself more comfortable in front of the fireplace. I left him laying in front of the cozy warmth and followed Rose down to her house. I stepped inside, china cabinets surrounded me, covering every wall. The china cabinets were filled with crystal balls, amethysts, different colored crystals, and, of course, the assorted dragons, fairies, unicorns, and Pegasus. Some were made of glass, others pewter with the crystals sitting on top, and some were ceramic. Rose loves her dust catchers. I couldn't help to feel relieved that I wasn't the one who had to clean all of her knick-knacks.

"Help yourself to some cookies," Rose said, snapping me out of my thoughts. "I picked up your favorite, Oreos. As you've already been told Bears taking me out tomorrow, so I want to give you a few things tonight. I'll be right back."

I scanned the kitchen and found a fat baby dragon

38

cookie jar. I tried not picture the shapes of her glasses and other dishes as I snagged a couple of cookies and sat down at the kitchen table. She returned a moment later with a big bag that smelled like Rosemary and made herself comfortable.

"I made these for you," she said as she pulled out several bunches of Rosemary tied with silver strings. "Like I said they're for protection, you can put them anywhere, and they'll last for a while. Keep the ones you don't use in the fridge, so they don't dry out."

"Thank you, Rose."

"That's not all," she reached into her pocket, "I also made you this."

She pulled out an amulet. The amulet was made out of a black leather pouch, sewn up with dark blue beads, and attached to a black beaded necklace. Three small crystals hung from the bottom.

"The crystals on the bottom are blue, green, and black tourmaline. Blue for communication and psychic awareness, green for creativity, prosperity, abundance, the green also represents the life energy of plants, and the black protects against negativity. I filled the pouch with a few things for protection also." She handed it to me. "You should keep it on you at all times."

I examined the amulet before putting it on. I could smell the rosemary through the pouch. "I don't know what to say, Rose, this is beautiful. Thank you."

Really, I didn't know what to say to her. Apparently this whole protection/rosemary thing was a newly added quirk of hers. I already had several crystals I still needed to unpack from her that carried different healing powers. I

39

stood up to give her a hug.

"There's one more thing."

I sat back down. I was ready to go home.

"I prepared the loft for Chase. He'll be staying here while I'm gone." Rose sat back in her chair.

So much for my vacation.

"I know you wanted some alone time, but Chase is a nice kid. You'll like him. Plus he loves Pumpkin and will take good care of her while I'm gone."

"I thought he lived with Max."

"He does, but the horses are over here, and this gives him his own house to stay in for a while. He's also offered to keep the house clean for me and help you out if you need anything. I know you haven't met him yet, and I'm not sure if you're going to meet him before I leave, so I'll describe him to you. He's tall with long blond hair he usually keeps tied back, blue eyes, and he's very smart and charming. He's kind of cute, and I believe he's somewhere in his twenties. He's not interested in girls right now, but there are a couple of girls focused on him. You shouldn't have to worry about that, though; he promised me he wouldn't have any company while I'm gone. He understands you want some peace and quiet this winter."

"That's fine Rose," I said, she was starting to ramble. "I'll keep an eye out for him."

"Good, I'm glad you're alright with it."

I wasn't sure if I was alright with it, but I didn't want to tell her no. She'd already done a lot for me.

"I think that's all," Rose said starting to stand up.

"Actually, before I leave I wanted to ask you why you're giving me this talisman." The rosemary I understood and it smelled good.

Rose thought about my question for a minute, "you're going to be alone in the middle of the woods and even though I like Max, I think he might have some weird Wuju surrounding him. He's also very interested in you, I could tell tonight at dinner. He was staring at you all night. Please be careful of him."

The talisman wouldn't fend off Max, but this was the second time tonight I'd been told to be careful around him.

"Do you know something about him that makes you feel that way?" I asked.

"No, I don't know much about him at all. He's attracted to you and it bothers me."

I laughed "I can handle him, Rose," maybe, "besides I thought you wanted me to have a man. What does Wuju mean?"

"Wuju is something I thought of while watching him tonight. I'm not sure it's a bad thing, but there's something he's not telling us like he's very secretive. I do want you to have a man. I'm just not sure if he's the right one. Chase might be a better match."

"Well, don't worry about it. I'm sure Max has better things to do than hang out around here."

"That's part of the problem. I'm not sure anyone knows what he does except for Chase, and he's not talking. Max might have all the time in the world to hang out with you."

I hoped she was wrong.

"What's Max's last name?" I stifled a big yawn. "And what time is your plane leaving?"

"In the late afternoon. We'll run your errands, then you

can drop me off. I know how much you like shopping."
Rose said jokingly. "It's Grey, Max Grey."

"Thanks." I gave Rose a hug and thought about how
much I hated shopping. "I'll be home. Come get me when
you're ready."

After checking on Lightning and making sure
everything was ready for the next morning, I trudged back
up to my house while staying alert for anything out of the
ordinary. I let Killer out, stoked the fire, kicked off my
shoes, and searched the house. No Max, no strange
intruders. I found some geographical maps of both
properties and printed them out. Getting information on
Max could wait until later, I was exhausted. I threw a few
things into my backpack, along with my camera, extra
bullets, and some food. I made sure my gun was still
stashed under my pillow and wondered if I was getting
paranoid. Pushing the thought aside, I set the alarm and
dropped into bed.

Chapter Four

At 4:00 am the next morning my alarm beeped annoyingly. I couldn't figure out why so I hit the snooze button, rolled over, and fell back to sleep. At 4:10 the alarm shrilled at me again and I realized I should have been out of the house already. I sat up and rubbed my face. I wanted to curse the thing that plagued my land. I pictured Max, he would work. This was my hideaway from the craziness of the world and my well being was being disrupted.

I tried to rise, but my body didn't want to move. Wonderful, my muscles ached from the intense exercises routine I put myself through the day before. I stretched, stumbled to my clothes, got dressed, gathered my stuff, and made it down the stairs without falling. I put some coffee in a thermos and called for Killer.

"Come on Killer. I know no one in their right mind would be up this early, but we have to go."

After a little coaxing, he followed me down to the barn. He had no interest in Pumpkin this morning; his brain seemed to be as sluggish as mine. Ace stood silently in his stall. The moon let enough light into the barn for me to see, and I had my talisman on. I took these as really good signs.

I hoisted the saddle and reins, strapped them on a sleepy Lightning, mounted her and set off for the bridge.

When we crossed over the stream I dismounted, got out my flashlight and maps, and then poured myself some coffee. I sat down, lit a smoke, and blearily scanned the maps. My body still hurt and my brain was still sleepy. I glanced at the bridge, sorely tempted to cross back over and go back to bed, but this was my home. I didn't want protection. I wanted to be left alone. Darkness settled over me. The treetops barely let in any light from the moon. I couldn't be sure if would find anything out here, or exactly what I was searching for, but I would sense it. I concentrated on the task before me, to find something, anything.

Almost positive this property belonged to Max meant I had to keep an eye out for him, and I had to take into consideration that his property covered a much bigger area than mine. I wasn't sure where to start.

I sat, searching the map for landmarks so I wouldn't get lost when I spotted a small picture of a house almost dead center in the property. I didn't find any roads, but I didn't have the best printout of the map either, and I was surprised I came across the house in the first place.

I drank another cup of coffee, slowly bringing my brain to life.

"Okay Killer, we're walking from here, keep your eyes open," I whispered through chattering teeth from the morning chill.

"We're going to follow the edge of the property, wrap around and come back down the other side. We need to avoid the house at all costs. Maybe we'll find something."

I led Lightning while moving the flashlight from right to left on the ground in front of me. I'd never done any tracking before, but I was confident I would know the difference between animal tracks, footprints, and something strange.

I took in the darkness around me and wished I could tell time by examining the stars. I didn't own a watch and forgot my cell phone at the house.

What seemed like hours later we stopped, the sun still hadn't risen. *Maybe this thing was just haunting my property.* Ready to head back I scanned my surroundings and realized I was lost. The forest surrounded me in a veil of surrealistic overtures, making every tree look like the next. Damn! I pulled out my map, some food, and coffee. I found my landmarks on the map but hadn't seen any on the walk. I hadn't paid any attention to the landmarks on our jaunt through the woods and wanted to kick myself for my lack of awareness. I wasn't sure what to do at this point so I leaned my head back against the tree I sat in front of and closed my eyes.

The next thing I knew the sun shined brightly on my face, creating a red glow under my eyelids. The sun's warmth brought me fully awake. I yawned and stretched before checking my map again. I searched for the sun between the trees and led the animals away from it. I only had to walk about a mile before I cleared the trees and there it was. I couldn't believe I'd been this close. The stream gurgled right in front of me, the bridge – nowhere in sight. Okay, so this morning didn't turn out quite as I planned. I closed my eyes, told myself not to panic and pictured this as an adventure.

I love to read books. Every chance I get I usually have a book in front of me. This seemed to be the perfect time to find out if I had any kind of imagination similar to my favorite authors.

I smiled to myself and closed my eyes for a moment. I was the lost maiden trying to get home to my prince before the big bad monster found me. Lightning was my trusty steed that ran as fast as the wind and Killer was my vicious wolf that would fight till the end. I imagined Max as my prince but scratched the idea right away.

Shaking my head I tried again with no prince involved. I had to save the queen from the evil wizard who was going to lock her in the dungeon. Lightning was my trusty steed and Killer was my big, bad wolf. The second scenario worked better for me. Feeling less panicked and considering writing a book I took on the role of a hero, hopped on my trusty steed, then headed upstream hoping I'd find the bridge soon.

I rode for a while with no success before coming to a shallow section of water. Lightning and I trudged through the stream and were hiking up the bank when I heard a loud whine. I glanced back; Killer paced the bank behind us with his tail tucked between his legs. With a long sigh, I jumped off Lightning and called to Killer a few times. He wanted nothing to do with the water, so much for my vicious wolf. Oh well, my imagination didn't seem to warrant any serious writing on my part anyway. I would leave that up to my favorite authors.

I cringed when I stepped into the stream. The icy water started to seep through my boots and jeans immediately.

Great! I was still lost and now I was going to freeze to death because I had to get my dog. I crossed the stream, coaxed Killer through the shallow water, finally got him across, and squished back up the bank. I had to get home now, my freezing wet pants glued themselves to my legs. I shook my legs and jumped up and down for a minute to get some feeling back in my feet. Tired and cold I yanked the map out of my jacket and found the area I thought I might be in. I smiled. If I was right my cozy cabin was close. I snatched up Lightning's reins, thinking I'd stay warmer if I walked, and had only taken a few steps when my skin began to crawl. My adrenaline soared and panic pulsed through my blood.

I searched the riverbank, turned around in a full circle and reached in my jacket pocket for my gun. Empty. My hand skimmed over my other pocket, empty too. I glanced at the pack on Lightning's back. Was my gun in the pack? I wanted my gun, yet I didn't want to take the time to look for it and I didn't want to make whatever was threatening me feel threatened enough to attack me. Crap. Why hadn't I kept my gun on me? I glanced over my shoulder but didn't see anything. I wanted to run; instead, I slowly moved my head searching the area around me one more time. I noticed Killer and Lightning patiently waiting. I grimaced. Was I losing my mind? Not even Lightning reacted to the invisible intruder. Did I really have two defective animals?

I cleared my head, even if I'd lost my mind I knew I had to move. Though my nerves stood on end, and my hands shook I started walking. Better to be a moving target. Right?

My gut kept telling me something circled me. Strange

47

shadowed blurs of movement contorted tree branches in my peripheral vision. As soon as I'd turn my head to get a good look the movement would be gone. I started to sidle up to Lightning to get my gun. Several things happened at once. My hand brushed Lightning's saddle an inch away from the pistol grip, a roof blurred through my vision beyond the trees, then something yanked my feet out from underneath me, and started running with me in tow.

I landed with a hard enough thud to knock the breath out of me. Once my lungs filled back up with air my body went into motion. My arm flailed, trying to grab a hold of the ground to slow me down. Whatever had me sped up, along with my heart. Don't panic, don't panic, I repeated to myself as a blur of trees and branches flew past me at a fast pace. I had to save myself. I twisted, noticed a tree coming toward me, and made a split-second decision to grab it and hold on for dear life. The tree came up fast, I twisted again and reached out for it. I was able to latch on the small trunk and wrap my arms tightly around the bottom. My nails bit into the bark. at the same time, my feet hit the ground and my body began to swing around due to the momentum of the twist. I saw what was going to happen next, but couldn't stop it. I commanded my arms to let go of the tree before my head made contact with the lower branch, but my arms wouldn't budge. I quickly turned my head, so I wouldn't smash face first into the branch, and felt a searing pain rage through my body.

I came around to a wet tongue on my face and attempted to brush it away, but an iron grip held my arm down. At least, I was warm again I thought as I slowly opened my eyes. I blinked a few times, blackness enveloped me. My heart slammed into my chest, I freaked out. I was blind. I jerked upright and my head spun; dizziness engulfed me, someone gently pushed me back down. I counted to twenty and inhaled deeply, the dizziness started to subside. The desire to know where I'd ended up, who had me and why I couldn't see encompassed me.

"Relax," Max said softly.

The situation was worse than I thought, Max found me. It would probably be easier fending off complete strangers.

"I'm blind," I whispered.

He chuckled. "You're not blind; I have a black cloth tied around your head, covering your eyes. I'm going to remove it slowly, so your eyes can adjust to the light without giving you a blinding headache. Are you ready?"

Relief flooded me.

"Yes."

He removed the cloth. I blinked my blurry eyes open. I was home, laying on my couch, with a fire roaring in the fireplace.

"How long have I been out?"

"We're not sure. Chase found you unconscious behind the barn this afternoon. He brought you up here and went into town to get the Doc. The Doc says you'll be fine, he left some pain killers for your head and some salve for your scrapes. No concussion."

"Where's Chase?" I asked, glancing around the room.

"He went back to my place. What happened? It looks like you were dragged all over the place."

"Where's Killer and Lightning?" I took my time sitting up and thought about what lies I would tell him next. I

49

shifted under the blanket that covered me and blushed. I was as naked as the day I was born. I touched the salve-covered cut on my hip and groaned, it was tender.

"Chase found Killer and Lightning in the barn right before he found you. Lightning's still in the barn and Killer's asleep by the fireplace."

I glanced at Killer and yawned, sleep sounded wonderful to me.

"I need to relax in a bath and get dressed. You can go home now, we'll talk later. Thanks for all your help."

Yep, bath, cozy clothes and sleep. I couldn't wait.

I stood up with the blanket, steadying myself against the couch for balance as a bout of dizziness hit me again.

"Does Rose know anything about this?"

"No, she's still out with Bear."

"Don't say anything to her. She's leaving tomorrow and I don't want her to worry." I made sure the blanket was fully wrapped around me and made my way towards the stairs picking up the bottle of painkillers on the way. I would need them later.

"Where's my backpack?"

Max wrapped his arm around my waist. "It's on your bed."

I tensed when Max's hip slid against mine. He was too close for my comfort zone.

"You really don't have to stay, I'll be fine."

His eyes narrowed into a grimace.

"I'm not leaving and you're too weak to kick me out. I'll start your bath and cook us some dinner. We can finish our conversation from yesterday. Remember I'm supposed to be protecting you. That's hard to do when you leave your house before the sun comes up without telling anyone where you're going."

He helped me up the stairs and sat me down on the bed before stomping into the bathroom. I rummaged through my backpack for my smokes as I listened to the bathtub fill up. I also found my gun where I left it, in Lightning's pack. I stashed the gun under my mattress. We were back to the protector thing again and even after today's events I didn't want him protecting me. I took a painkiller out of the bottle, bit it in half and gulped it down with some water.

I didn't say anything when he came out of the bathroom. I just marched the best I could pass him locking the door behind me. I let the blanket fall to the floor and examined my damaged body. I had some scrapes on my lower back from where my shirt and jacket road up while being dragged, and my butt, arms, and shoulders glowed pink. The nastiest injury was the one on my hip. It looked like a small, sharp tree branch or rock sliced through my skin. I had a knot on the side of my head that hurt to the touch, but, all in all, I was just sore and dirty. The salve sat on the counter-top reminding me Max had been in the bathroom to help me. A small bout of depression hit me from getting ambushed. Well, at least, I'm not paranoid, I thought to myself, something was stalking me. I had the war wounds to prove it. I climbed into the tub, stretched, and promptly fell asleep.

I awoke, startled, to loud banging on the door.

"Montana!" Bang, bang, bang. "Montana! Are you alright?" Bang, bang.

"Stop banging on my door! I'm fine and you're giving me a headache!" I yelled as my head started throbbing to

51

the beat of my heart.

"Dinners ready. Do I need to come in and get you?" Max said quietly and passionately.

"Give me a couple of minutes."

I closed my eyes for a minute and took several deep breaths, all of this attention I was getting lately was driving my crazy.

A cup of coffee waited for me on my dresser when I finally made my way out of the bathroom. I took it as a good sign, he wasn't too mad. The last thing I needed to deal with was a mad Max. Giggling at my joke, I found an ashtray, lit a smoke, and drank the coffee. I dressed in some gray sweats and warm fluffy hot pink socks before heading downstairs.

Chapter Five

We stared at each other while we ate, or should I say while he ate. My stomach growled, but at the same time, I couldn't eat any food. I also didn't feel like talking. I pushed my food around my plate while trying to conjure up a plan. I didn't want to lie to him again, but I also didn't want to tell him the truth about what happened to me today or where I'd disappeared to. My thoughts were a jumbled mess. So many unanswered questions kept popping into my head. What was that thing? Why did the animals not sense it? Where did it come from? Why me? I needed time to think without him around.

After dinner, I refilled my coffee and went into the living room. I settled into my chair, took the other half of the painkiller and lit a smoke. I heard the dishes clanking and the water running in the kitchen, which gave me a few more minutes to think. My mind was a blank, though. I couldn't come up with any excuse or lie for what happened to me. I'd have to wing it when Max started asking me questions. Maybe I could avoid his interrogation until I had the answers I needed.

Max sauntered into the living room carrying a cup of

java and sat on the couch. "Can I have one of your smokes?"

I handed him the pack.

"Look, Max, you really don't need to stay. I'm just a little sore and need some rest. I'll be here for the rest of the night. I'm taking Rose to the airport in the morning and I'll be home for the next few days taking care of business."

"You're beautiful. I love those hot pink socks."

My jaw dropped. I didn't expect the conversation to head in that direction and was at a loss for words. I started laughing so hard I couldn't stop. Almost every time I had a nervous reaction I would laugh, and Max made me nervous more often than not. When I finally got my breath back I glanced up at Max.

"You're crazy Max, you need to leave. Rose wouldn't be happy if she found you here in the morning." And neither would I.

"Give it up Montana. I'm not going anywhere. I stopped by early this morning with Chase and you weren't here. We went to the barn and Lightning was gone. I waited for you to come back. When Chase walked into the house with you all scratched up and unconscious I became concerned. After he put you on the couch and I made sure you were alright I got pissed that you left the house without me and got injured. I'm staying tonight. I'll be gone before Rose comes to get you, but I'll be back before you get home. Are you ready to tell me what happened today?"

"No, I have to wrap my head around this." I glared at him. I couldn't understand why he wouldn't just go away.

"If you insist on staying you can sleep on the couch. Goodnight." I left him sitting in the living room and fell into bed fully dressed, which was probably a good thing.

Max had his arms wrapped tightly around my waist, he snuggled behind me, sound asleep. I pictured pushing him off the bed and grinned, but his hold was solid and I could barely move.

I laid in my spot not moving an inch for a few minutes contemplating on how to get out of his vice grip, while enjoying the closeness of his body at the same time, before prying his hands apart. My emotions were too wound up when it came to Max. I wanted him to go away, I didn't want to enjoy his touch. I was happy being single.

"What are you doing?" He whispered in my ear, creating little shivers that floated over my skin.

"Let me go Max."

"What if I don't want to?" He asked, but rolled over onto his back anyway.

I rolled onto my back before flipping to my stomach. Hot licks of pain ran over my road rash skin, the slash on my hip started to throb, my behind ached to the touch.

"Why aren't you on the couch?" I'd just about given up on getting rid of him.

"You were having nightmares."

"I don't remember having nightmares."

"Ah, I'm sure that's because once I crawled into bed with you the nightmares stopped."

I didn't believe him for a minute. I eyed the clock, 7 a.m. I might as well start my day. I scooted over to the edge of the bed still on my stomach and tried to think of a graceful way to get out of bed. Finding no gracefulness to getting up I swung my feet to the floor, pushed myself up with my hands, and cringed when I stood. I stumbled into the bathroom to check out my damaged body and shower, ignoring Max, who was laughing into his pillow. One glance at him showed me he was, at least, shirtless and I didn't want to know or think about what other parts of clothing he didn't wear under the covers.

I tugged off my shirt and sweats and examined the scratch marks on my lower back and the gash on my hip. The gash had a red, angry flare around it, but didn't look infected. My behind felt like it should be black and blue, but I didn't see any bruises. I grabbed at my socks and when I peeled them off I noticed black and blue hand marks on both of my ankles, or what I assumed were hand marks. The bruises seemed more elongated than a normal hand print, which seemed wrong. Maybe from the hands slipping? I rubbed my fingers over the prints coming to the conclusion some kind of psychopathic person had grabbed me.

My head rested against the shower wall thinking of how to fit some of the pieces together when I heard the door open.

"Now, what do you want?"

"I brought you some coffee and painkillers." Max said, sitting down on the edge of the tub.

I opened the shower door a crack and peeked out. He wore a black thermal long sleeved shirt and blue jeans. I stared at the five buttons on his shirt and imagined unsnapping them and running my fingers over his chest.

"I'm getting out now."

"Would you like me to hand you a towel?" He asked,

grinning wide.

"No, I'd like you to go somewhere else."

He tried to pout, but the grin still reached his eyes. "I'll be downstairs if you need anything."

I waited until the door closed behind him, jumped out of the shower and turned the lock on the doorknob. I hurried, put the salve on my scrapes, got dressed, threw on some makeup, and fluffed my hair with my fingers. The bump on my head felt smaller but still throbbed.

Slinking into my bedroom and looking around to make sure I was alone I took some pictures of my ankles. Satisfied I had some evidence I swallowed half a pain killer and went downstairs. I found Max standing in my kitchen looking lost.

"What are you doing?"

"Attempting to cook breakfast, but I can't find anything in your kitchen to cook. Tell me again why you only have protein drinks."

I turned on the TV and started rummaging through my yoga disks, I needed a good stretch.

"I usually don't get hungry until around lunch."

I found the DVD I was looking for and put it in the machine.

"You do know breakfast is the most important meal of the day," He replied, watching me closely.

"Hence the drinks," I carefully began stretching.

"There's bacon in the freezer, help yourself. As far as eggs go, I won't be getting any until I find someone with chickens. Fresh are the best." I didn't consider myself a health nut. I just didn't like supporting big corporations if I didn't have too, besides fresh eggs trumped store bought eggs anytime.

"Chase knows someone. I'll mention it to him."

"You mean the ghost kid?" I snickered.

"He's real. Is that helping?" Max had defrosted the bacon in the microwave and now it sizzled in the pan.The smell of bacon frying made my stomach growl.

"The yoga? It has to, I'm driving today and don't want to take a ton of painkillers. I also don't want to explain why I'm stiff and sore to Rose."

"So why aren't you taken?" Max asked as he sat on the couch with a big plate of bacon and Killer on his heels drooling. I think he cooked the whole package.

I thought about his question as I watched him slip some of the bacon to Killer. I wasn't expecting the discussion to turn to me again.

"I'm a selfish person Max. I don't like to share and I've been told I can be too blunt in my honesty. I tend to hurt other people's feelings easily and I'm not a relationship kind of girl. I like my independence."

"You're beautiful and sexy, even though you've lied to me several times since I met you."

I ignored him and finished my workout. An uneasy quiet engulfed my living room. I glanced at Max, his gaze was glued to my ankles. My sweats had ridden up my legs during my stretching and the hand prints glared an ugly purple color on my white skin.

His eyes flashed angrily. "Talk to me. Tell me what happened." He picked me up and set me on the couch so he could examine the bruises better. "These are hand prints." He touched them gently, sending an electric current up my legs and into my belly.

My heart started racing and all of a sudden I wanted him to kiss me. I slid back against the couch as fast as I could and quickly covered my ankles, willing my heart to slow down and my mind to come back to reality.

I scowled at him. "If you must know, I took Lightning out yesterday morning for an early ride and was on my way home when I realized someone was watching me. I stopped and dismounted so I could scope out the area. The animals didn't react to anything abnormal, so I decided I would walk them the rest of the way home. I was almost out of the woods when someone or something yanked my feet out from under me and started running, dragging me."

I leaned toward him and looked him in the eyes. "I didn't see anything Max. I didn't see it coming and I didn't see what had a hold of me."

I closed my eyes, visualizing the moment. "The shadows from the leaves seemed off and I'd catch a glimpse of the sun filtering through the trees." I took a deep breath and exhaled, opening my eyes I sat back. "I can't explain it, like a shadow blending in with its surroundings? I saw a tree coming toward me at close range and grabbed it. Whatever had me let me go and I swung around with enough force to hit my head on the bottom branch."

Okay, so I didn't tell him the whole truth, he didn't need to know I was most likely on his property scouting.

"Where was your gun?"

My face lit up with surprise, his lips twitched the tiniest bit in amusement.

"Yes, I know you have a gun Montana and I know you carry it when you go out. Where was it?"

"It was in Lightning's pack. I forgot to take it out when

59

I dismounted and I didn't want that thing to feel threatened enough to attack me if I reached for it. I thought I would see it coming."

What could I say? I've never had to reckon my property before or keep a constant eye on my life, all of this was new to me.

He got up, started a fire, and stood in front of the blaze.

Thank goodness he didn't ask me about my wet shoes.

I walked over to him. "Rose will be here soon and I have to get ready. Max, is anyone else in danger here?"

He turned and pulled me closer him, wrapping his arms loosely around my back.

"No Montana. This thing seems to only be interested in you. I need to find out why. Promise me you'll keep your gun on you at all times."

He kissed my neck, sending flames shooting down to my toes.

"You should forgive Killer." He breathed across my hair. "He can't sense this thing, no animals can. I'm sure he would protect you if he could."

I laughed, nervousness wracked my body from being in Max's arms and I didn't like the desire his closeness evoked in me. "He won't be able to protect me if you keep feeding him all that bacon. He'll be too fat."

I picked up his plate, only three slices of bacon remained, poured myself some more coffee, and climbed the stairs to my bedroom. I sat on my bed and lit a smoke, willing my nerves to calm before Rose arrived.

Chapter Six

When I went back downstairs Max was gone. Reveling in the silence, I picked up my shopping list and rechecked it as I went through every room to make sure I had written down everything I needed. I added binoculars, a small notepad, and a folder. I wanted to document everything that happened and keep notes. I knew Rose would be showing up any minute, so I ran back upstairs, which I immediately regretted, took half a painkiller, found my gun, and stashed both of them in my backpack. Next I checked to make sure my ankle pictures were still on the memory stick in my camera. I took the card out and stashed it in my backpack also. I was having trust issues.

"Come in, Rose," I said as I sat down to put on my boots.

Rose bustled in. "I'm finally ready to go, or as ready as I'll ever be this year. We need to stop by my house and get my luggage then we'll hit the road."

"Relax Rose, take a deep breath, I still have to let Killer out and give him a bone, he's staying home this time."

I stood on the deck waiting for Killer to finish his

61

business and let my eyes drift over the landscape. I released a sigh of relief. I didn't see Max anywhere and nothing seemed out of place. As soon as Killer finished up he ran inside and planted himself in front of the fireplace.

"Be good Killer, I'll be back tonight." I gave him an extra-large rawhide bone to chew on for the day and scratched behind his ears.

Rose and I drove in silence for the next hour, both of us deep in our own thoughts. When we arrived at my first destination Rose looked over at me.

"I'm staying in the truck" she said. "You make shopping into a marathon race and I don't want to get left behind."

"I don't blame you, I'll be right back."

I grabbed my shopping bags and got right to it. Rose was right, I entered the store and raced through the aisles. My motto, go in and get out as quickly as possible. Stores make me claustrophobic, the aisles are too narrow, and too many people liked to gather and talk to each other in them, creating endless roadblocks to maneuver through. I rushed out of the store in no time flat. We did this for all of the other stops I had to make and then drove towards the airport.

"We're early," Rose said. "Let's stop for some coffee and pie first."

I pulled into the first parking lot I found. The street leading to the airport had restaurants and hotels on both sides. We parked at an all-night coffee shop and claimed a booth by the window, ordered coffee with key lime pie and dug in.

"Give me all the juicy details," I said to Rose, knowing she understood what I was talking about because her face turned bright red.

"We're just having a good time together."

"Is the relationship serious?"

"Well, he didn't want me to leave and I don't want to leave either, so I guess it's as serious as it's going to get."

I grinned, their affair could get more serious if she let loose, she'd been alone for a very long time. I watched her as I finished my pie. She purposely dressed down today in jeans, a blue sweater, and brown boots. She'd pulled her hair back in her normal braid, but left the sparkling hair clips out. I knew this was how she was going to be dressed during her visit with her kids and it made me sad she felt like she had to be someone else so she wouldn't embarrass her family. She should be able to stay up in the mountains with me, everyone up there liked her just the way she was, including Bear. A smile spread across my face.

"What are you smiling about?"

"I'm just happy Bear likes you for who you really are," I said as I waved for the waitress. "I wish you could stay."

"Yeah, me too. Bear's a good guy. He's going to get in touch with you after Thanksgiving for the meeting, is that alright?"

"That's fine with me, I'll cook dinner for him or something." Hopefully the psycho creature wouldn't hanging around my house by then. Because honestly, I didn't think it was a psycho human anymore after thoroughly examining the mutated hand prints the thing left on my ankles.

I ordered a whole Key Lime pie to go before we drove

63

the last mile to the airport. We sat at the toll both waiting to pay the fee when I noticed a tear slide down Roses cheek. I gave Rose a questioning glance.

"I'm alright," she sighed as she stared out the passenger side window. "I'm going to miss the mountains, you know my family isn't that bad, they just want me to grow up."

"No worries Rose, I like your family, they just need to relax a bit and give you a break. You've done your job raising them."

"They're professionals," we both laughed.

Rose's family were wealthy, successful, suit wearing, briefcase carrying professionals. They leaned closer to the stuffy side if anyone asked me, but since no-one ever did I kept the thought to myself.

I found a close parking space in the terminal and we both dug Rose's luggage out from underneath all of my stuff. We hauled it into the airport and gave it to the lady at the counter, she printed out Roses tickets, and we took the escalator to security. I handed Rose her Christmas present, which I hoped she'd unwrap on the plane. The small package contained a small pewter dragon wrapped around a ruby colored thin crystal I'd put on a long chain for her to wear while she was in Cali. She could easily hide the necklace under her sweaters, so it wouldn't be seen. We gave each other a big hug and I watched her go through security. I cringed, I was now officially alone with Max and ghost boy.

I made one last stop at a Mexican food restaurant on the drive out of town to pick up a spinach and cheese blue corn enchilada with green chili, sour cream, and three

64

sopapillas. I needed some comfort food for the next couple of days.

My mouth watered as the scent of the enchilada wafted through the truck, and my stomach growled. I was so distracted by the thought of kicking my feet up by a nice roaring fire, reading a book, and eating, that by the time I pulled into my driveway I'd forgotten about retrieving my gun out of my purse for protection. I had my dinner and pie in my hands and was jogging up the steps to my deck when I came to an abrupt stop. A nest of leaves built similar to an underground burrowing animal rested in front of my door. I didn't hesitate; I unlocked my front door, avoided the mess as much as possible, stepped in, and slammed the door behind me, locking it. An icy numbness rapidly consumed my shaking hands, goose bumps slithered over my skin. I wasn't hungry anymore.

I set my food down on the counter and flew to the back door, still locked, good. I stood there for a moment holding my breath then slowly opened the door and peeked outside. There, on the ground sat another nest of leaves. I closed the door and re-locked it, my whole body vibrated in disbelief. I wrapped my arms tightly around my chest in an attempt to stop the shakes, calm down and clear my head from the numbness that had taken over. Killer rubbed his side against my leg. I slid down the door, wrapped my arms around his big, thick, neck and I willed myself not to cry.

After a few minutes of resting my head in Killers fur, I realized he needed to go out. I needed to brave the outdoors too, the sun was setting and I needed to grab my gun and my bags out of the truck. I also needed to take pictures of the nests.

"Wait here Killer I have an idea." I ran upstairs to get my camera before finding Killers leash and collar.

"I'm sorry to have to do this to you boy, but I want you as close to me as possible." I secured his collar and shortened his leash. "We're going to have to watch our step when we go out front, I want to get some pictures before the nests become disturbed."

We managed to get back outside without causing too much damage. Killer avoided the nests and whined at the sight of them. I snagged the gun out of my backpack. Feeling a little safer I gave Killer some slack to do his business but didn't let go of the leash. I put the memory card back in my camera and grabbed everything I could carry out of my truck. The rest could wait until daylight. I snapped some pictures of the nests, went back inside, and proceeded to search my house, making sure it was locked down tight.

I heated my food, started a fire, and sat down on the couch before turning on my favorite zombie movie for a distraction. I also wondered where the hell my protector was. A knock on the door rattled my nerves, Max stepped inside.

"Re-lock the door behind you." I hadn't heard or sensed him coming up the drive. That's how freaked out I was.

He gave me a questioning glance, sat down beside me and directed his attention to the movie.

I ignored him, the adrenaline rush from earlier faded and left me frazzled, exhausted, and in no mood for conversation.

Eventually, I made my weary limbs get off the couch

for coffee, pie, and a painkiller. I put my uneaten dinner in the fridge and cut two slices of pie, one for me and one for Max, who was still in silent mode. I handed him the pie and we continued to watch the movie.

I stirred the next morning in my own bed. The other side of the bed was empty but rumpled. I glared at the dent from Max's head lingering on the pillow. He'd slept in my bed again. What did Max not understand about sleep on the couch or go away?

I closed my eyes and stretched out; I was tempted to stay in bed for the rest of the day. I didn't want to deal with anything. I imagined Max leaving, my home being safe again, and snuggled deeper under the blankets. The smell of coffee, eggs, and bacon awakened my senses and brought me back to reality. My stomach growled, I threw off the covers and sat up.

Apparently Max thought it necessary to take off most of my clothes last night. I planted my feet on the floor, wearing only a tee-shirt, boxers, and fluffy pink socks. I smirked, I was sleeping with the guy, without the sex, so I why should I complain.

I slipped on a robe and a moment later stepped into the solarium Max was no longer in the house. His energy still lingered in the air, but my internal sensors told me he'd left. Curious as to who was cooking in my kitchen, I rounded the corner and almost ran into ghost boy.

"You startled me." Ghost boy said, putting his hand over his heart. "I'm Chase." He held out his hand to me. "I hope you don't mind I'm here, but Max needed to run some errands and didn't want you to be left alone."

Great, another protector, a cute one, but nonetheless. I plastered a smile on my face. "It's nice to finally meet you."

"Max said you only eat fresh eggs." He sauntered back into the kitchen. I followed him. "I know a lady who has chickens, so I brought some over, eggs not chickens. She told me to tell you that if you ever need a chicken to let me know."

The thought of owning a live chicken or having one killed made me squeamish.

"I will, thanks."

"I hope you're hungry. I made breakfast and was going up to check on you when you almost ran into me. Max says you don't eat breakfast, but I figured I'd try anyway."

"Breakfast sounds great." I poured myself some coffee and wondered what else Max told Chase about me.

Chase loaded up some plates for both of us and we sat down at the guest island.

"I also took the liberty of bringing the rest of your stuff in from the truck. I set up Killer's auto pet feeder in the solarium, and I took Killer out with me when I cleaned up the mess outside."

"Thanks. Any idea what kind of nest sat on my doorstep?" I already liked Chase; he was boyishly cute, polite, and charming.

"No, and Max didn't say anything. He took some pictures of those things in front of your doors and left very unhappy."

I put my plate in the sink and refilled my coffee. "So what's on the agenda for today?" I giggled. "Are you supposed to lock me in my room or something until Max

68

gets back?"

"No," Chase laughed. "Even though I think he'd be thrilled if I did. You're the first female I've seen him attach himself to since I've known him."

"And how long is that?"

"About five years, he likes you. I can see why."

I raised my eyebrows. I didn't want to go there, besides Chase didn't know me well enough to make that particular comment.

"Well, I'll make life easy for you, I have some work I need to get done today, so I'll be a good girl and stay inside."

"I appreciate your kindness." He replied with a big grin.

"Make yourself at home."

I found Killer in his usual spot by the fireplace and gave him a pet before heading back upstairs to get ready for the day.

After I showered and got dressed, I cleaned my room and booted up my laptop. I checked on all of my investments, putting myself in a comatose state of mind. When I started to yawn I closed the computer window I worked in and picked up my camera. I spent the next couple of hours printing the photos of my ankles, writing notes, and doing research. I couldn't find anything about the unusual nests or the hand prints. Needing a break, I headed back downstairs for more coffee.

Chase sat on the floor with his back against the couch and Killers head lying on his legs, glued to the TV. My second favorite zombie movie held his attention. I probably could've snuck outside and he would never have known. I

69

moved silently into the kitchen, refilled my coffee, and popped some popcorn. Resident Evil was just what the doctor ordered. I sat down next to Chase. Startled, he almost jumped out of his skin. His knees flew up clocking Killer in the jaw, making Killer jump too. Chase's glazed over eyes stared at me like I was a zombie. I busted out in giggles.

"I take it you haven't seen this episode before," I said, hitting the pause button.

He shook his head. "No, I haven't and you scared the crap out of me."

"If you forgive me I'll share my popcorn with you."

"It's a deal." He dug into the popcorn.

By the time the movie ended, I was itching to ask Chase a ton of questions, I also longed to go outside and walk around or go riding.

"Resident Evil is awesome, mind if I play another disk?"

"Help yourself. Any idea when Max might be back or where he went?"

"No idea."

"Why is he looking into this? This situation isn't his problem."

"He works in things like this."

"What does that mean?"

"You like him, don't you."

Why did everyone always change the subject on me? I blew out a breath. "I don't know, I've got more work to do," being stuck in the house was even worse than shopping.

I sat back down in front of my laptop, lit a smoke, and

70

put Max's name into more than one search engine on the Internet, coming up empty. Getting depressed, I closed my laptop, found a good book, and went back downstairs to hang out with Chase. We ended up watching almost all of my Resident Evil movies and eating the rest of my pie for dinner. Max never showed that night, which was a huge relief.

I left Chase absorbed in Alice's chaos and went to bed.

Chapter Seven

I woke up in an excellent mood, my body didn't ache anymore and Max hadn't slept in my bed. I felt like I could conquer anything and everything life threw at me. I stretched and wandered downstairs for my first cup of coffee. I held in a giggle when I heard Chase snoring. I peeked into the living room, his head stuck out of a bundle of blankets, Killer snuggled up to him, similar to a big tumor on his side. I tiptoed into the kitchen, poured coffee, headed back upstairs, took a quick shower, and got dressed. When I strolled back downstairs Chase's blurry eyed gaze glanced up at me, he gripped his coffee like his life depended on it.

"I take it you didn't get much sleep last night?" I asked, trying not to laugh. He looked pretty bad.

"I've been so busy lately; I haven't had time to watch any movies. Resident Evil rocks!"

"How many did you watch?"

"Almost all of them."

I laughed at the thought of him and his movie marathon. "Maybe you should slow down a bit. You can borrow them anytime."

"Thanks, I need another cup of java," He said, rotating his now, empty cup upside down.

I refilled both of our cups and sighed. "I need to get out today. You're more than welcome to come with me, but one whole day stuck in this house is enough."

"That's cool, if you don't mind me using your shower real quick we'll figure out something to do."

"You're not afraid Max will get upset with you?"

"Nah, he was supposed to come back last night and he didn't. Besides, I could use some fresh air too."

While Chase took his shower I busied myself picking up and checking my messages, something I should probably do every day, but hadn't bothered to do since I'd been here. Rose called to say thank you for the necklace and she'd call back on Thanksgiving. My sister called sounding like her happy normal self and my mom called. They all promised to call me back on Thanksgiving and reminded me to turn my phone on that day. I cringed, Thanksgiving Day would soon be upon me and I'd forgotten all about it. I needed to go shopping. I wanted to donate food to the shelters anonymously.

"Hey, Chase, how would you like to go shopping with me today?" I asked as he came trotting down the hallway.

"Sure."

I told him my plan and made sure the chamber in my gun was loaded while Chase put Killer's leash on. As soon as we opened the door Killer growled, we both looked outside, the blood drained from our faces. Chase closed the door and we gazed at each other for a moment, not sure what to say.

I cleared my throat, "I'm going to get my camera and

take some pictures. We need to check the back door too."

"Afterward, I'll check the barn. Do you still want to go shopping?" Chase asked.

Hell yes! I still wanted to go shopping, well, not necessarily shopping, but I wanted out of my house badly. I wasn't in the right mindset to deal with this thing right now, and might never be.

"Yes, we'll get pictures, check the barn, and let Max deal with the rest if he shows up."

I grabbed my camera, we tugged the door ajar and I scoped out the area around the front of the house and deck. Killer growled low, under his breath. I didn't see anything and my radar didn't ding, so we carefully stepped outside. Another nest sat in front of the door. This nest was built bigger than the first, with dead bugs and dead birds tucked inside the cave like structure. *An offering? For me?* My gut said I was right. I shivered, these nests were the creepiest things I'd ever seen and chilled me to the bone. I took as many pictures, from all angles, as I could stand then proceeded to the back door.

Apparently, whatever had become enthralled with me had nothing better to do with its time than stalk me in its own unorthodox way. The nest by the back door took up almost a half of the width of the frame, stood, at least, a foot tall, and was more intricately made than the dwelling on the front deck. Dead bugs, birds, and a couple of squirrels were crammed into the burrow for good measure.

My gag reflex flared, I came close to emptying the coffee out of my stomach. The thing had taken its time-twisting twigs and branches together into a cone shape pocket, leaves inter-weaved around and through the cone to

74

block wind and weather. Dead birds lay against the back of the nest, dead bugs lay haphazardly around the inside, and the dead squirrels rested at the front of the entrance.

My heart beat double time, my skin crawled, and I had to keep swallowing hard to keep the bile from rising into my throat. I needed to get out of here and I didn't have to glance at Chase to know that he was ready to get out of dodge too. I tried to keep my hands from shaking as I snapped off more pictures of the dead creatures inside the nest.

Killer stopped growling once we stepped off the deck to check on Pumpkin and the horses. After making sure, Pumpkin and Lightning were alright we locked up the barn. Ace's stall stood empty, I figured Max had him. I shook my head, amazed at how often I looked for Max's horse to tell me if he was around. I had to stop doing that.

We both heaved a big sigh of relief once we loaded into my truck and hit the road. Chase closed his eyes as soon as we turned off the dirt lane and onto the pavement. He slept for the whole trip into the city, which was fine by me, it gave me time to ponder my predicament, and he would need his energy to keep up with my power shopping. If we were lucky we'd only have to stop at a few stores. I glanced at the horizon, big, puffy clouds were beginning to cover the mountains and dim the sun, snow would start falling soon. I stepped on the gas to make good time and stopped in front of the first organic food store we arrived at.

I nudged Chase, "Time to wake up sleeping beauty."

He opened his eyes and squinted, "I need coffee, I was having a really bad dream." He blinked a couple of times then jolted fully awake. "Oh shit, it wasn't a dream was

75

it!?"

"I wish it was a dream. Come on we'll get some lattes. Do you have any idea what is making itself at home at my house?"

"You need to talk to Max, I'm sure he knows. If I knew I'd tell you."

"I will." The next time I see him.

We ordered our lattes and I gave him the list for the deli.

"I'm going to get the other things and meet you at the cashiers."

We parted ways and I sped walked through the aisles. I bought the store out of corn, potatoes, yams, stuffing, and cranberry jelly then piled most of the pumpkin pies the store had left in my cart. I stopped for whipped cream and tea bags, put all of those in my basket and almost ran into Chase rounding an aisle. For some reason, I couldn't sense him as well as everyone else I knew. I briefly wondered why as we waited for the cashier to total everything up.

We loaded the bags into the tool box in the back of my truck and stopped at two more stores before we had enough goodies for the shelters. Starving, we bought burgers and fries from the nearest drive-through restaurant and sat in the parking lot to eat. While we ate I put my hair up under a big floppy hat and changed out my sunglasses for some big face covering ones.

My face still appeared to be newsworthy from winning the lottery and I was getting tired of it. I had also helped enough small businesses out that newspapers constantly wanted the next story and a few news shows wanted to put me on the air. I sighed. When reporters dug in their claws they never seemed to retract them. I wanted to be able to give without being the hero of the moment.

"How do I look?" I asked Chase.

"Goofy," He said, laughing.

I've always believed if you were going to give to a charity, then you should give to that charity, without having to fill out the paperwork for the purpose of getting your money back on your taxes. I didn't want my money back, I just wanted to be able to drop the food off without being recognized, and since this was my first time doing it I was sure I needed a disguise. I moved the rear-view mirror so I could check out my disguise. I did look goofy. I briefly fantasized about wearing the get up at home and the psycho creature leaving because it thought I was someone else, but knew that would be too easy.

"We're going to stop at the back doors, drop off the food, ring the bell, and leave. We need to do this as fast as possible so we won't be seen." I said as we came up on the first shelter.

"I know you want to stay anonymous, but wouldn't leaving money be easier?"

"It would, but I'm not a very trusting person. I feel better knowing the shelters have food to serve the homeless in a nice warm environment. Ready?" I parked as close to the curb as I could. "Picture this as an adventure."

I put the truck in neutral and left it running. We jumped out and placed the food by the back door. I climbed back in the truck and put it in first gear while Chase rang the bell. When the doorknob turned he jumped into the truck. I hit the gas, driving away from the building. Shock registered on the man's face when he noticed the food surrounding the steps. Giving stirred a deep warmth in my heart.

Chase grinned, "How far to the next shelter?"

"Not far."

We made a game out of delivering the food to the shelters by timing ourselves. Once we had our initial time we would try to beat it at each new shelter we went to.

"Are you going to keep any of this food?" Chase asked as we reached our last destination.

"No." I pulled up to the curb. "We've got a problem."

"What's that?" He asked right before he noticed it. "Oh hell, the shelters surrounded by a fence and the whole front of the building has windows."

"How do you want to play this?

He considered the problem for a minute. "We have to go through the gate. Maybe we'll get lucky and the back porch will be windowless."

"This stop needs to excel our best time." I adjusted my hat, "are you ready?"

He rubbed his hands together and rummaged around behind us for a few bags of food. "Ready."

I opened the gates and drove through like I belonged there. I coasted to the back of the building. The back doors stood wide open. "Damn!" I made a u-turn and idled by the front door. Barred windows graced both sides of the entrance. "Go!"

Chase raced to the small enclosure with all of his bags as I raced to the back of the truck to get more; we grabbed as much as we could and put it on the front porch. We'd just snatched the last load out of the truck when an older priest dressed in clergy attire opened the door.

"What are you doing out here?" He asked in a low calm voice, almost tripping over the bags of groceries.

Chase and I ran up to him at the same time, shoved the rest of the goodies in his arms, and piled back into the truck. My heart was thumping with excitement as I yanked the gearshift into drive, flooring it through the side streets to my last stop.

"Wait here, I'll be right back."

I jogged into the store, rummaged around for my favorite zombie movies, paid the cashier, and jogged back to the truck.

Chase hadn't moved. I placed the bag in his lap and veered onto the interstate, last destination home.

"Montana."

"Ah, he speaks."

"That was the most fun I've had in a long time."

"I was starting to get worried about you Chase. You've been, like a zombie for a while." I replied, chuckling.

"When the priest came out of the shelter I felt totally busted. My first thought was we're going to jail. It just took time for my brain to come to the understanding that we didn't do anything wrong." His whole body shook for a second or two, and then he burst out laughing. "When can we do it again? Did we beat our best time?"

Relief washed over me. "I have no idea if we beat our time; I was motivated on getting us out of there. We'll figure out something new for Christmas if you're around."

"Oh, I'll be around."

We both laughed as he went through his bag of goodies. "Are all of these for me?"

"It's a thank you gift."

"Thanks, Montana." He fell silent for a moment. "What is it like winning the lottery?"

"What else has Max told you about me?" I countered.

"Everything he thought I should know with the promise I wouldn't tell anyone else. He said he'd kill me if I did. My lips are sealed."

"I'm going to keep you to that promise."

"Fair enough, so how does it feel?"

"It's great not having to worry about bills anymore and I get to help more people now, but it sucks to constantly be bothered by people and charities that want me to give." I chuckled. "Plus both men and women kept asking me out for dates. Getting away from the unnecessary attention is one of the reasons I moved to the mountains."

"Maybe some of those men actually wanted to get to know you."

"Sure, along with the women." I replied, distracted, huge snowflakes hit the windshield heavily, swirling snow began to glue itself to the road. I flipped on my headlights when low bearing clouds started to creep over us and slowed down to a crawl. We drove the rest of the way home through the intense white out. The whole time Chase was either bent forward or hanging his head out the window, making sure we didn't run off the road.

"Turn, turn now, there's your road."

I turned, slid, over-corrected and we spun around in a 360 before we stopped.

"Well, at least, we're facing the right direction," I said, making sure my heart hadn't stopped with the truck. I've driven in many snow storms and knew what I was doing, but sometimes nature had different plans. I hadn't expected the pavement to ice over this soon.

"Help me put the beast in four wheel drive and we'll try to make the drive to the house."

Setting the four wheel drive on my truck wasn't an easy task. The locks needed to be rotated on the outside tires and the locks were frozen. After melting some of the ice with my lighters, we managed to click the locks on four wheel drive. I immediately turned on headlights and the heat full blast to unfreeze us when we climbed back into the cab. I put the truck into gear and we slowly crawled up my dirt road. Chase hung his head out the passenger side window, telling me where the ruts on his side of the road were. I hung my head out of the drivers side window, keeping an eye out for ruts as well. We made it a little over two miles before I plowed into a snow drift that covered a deep rut.

"I've got to get this road paved!" I screamed as I put the truck in reverse, cranked the wheel left and tried to ease us out of the hole. I accomplished sliding the rear-end to the right. I cranked the wheel to the right and put the truck in first gear hoping to catch some fresh snow for traction, but all I managed was another slide, and to sink us deeper into the snow drift. I cursed under my breath. My arms, hands, and finger muscles were rigid from gripping the wheel.

Chase gave me a moment before he began unhooking my fingers from the steering wheel, they were locked up tight.

"We're going to have to walk from here," He said. "Just so you know Rose did try to get the road graded, but the company couldn't get out here in time. They were mega

81

busy."

"Okay. Fine," I flexed my fingers a few times to get the cramps out. "I haven't put any emergency clothes in my truck yet." My mind had been on other things. "Your right, we're going to have to walk the rest of the way."

The snow fell faster now and darkness settled over us like a thick, black blanket. My skin pricked with unease. I picked up my purse and took out my gun.

"Stay close to me; hold my belt loop or something. I'm not sure what's out there and I don't want to get separated."

I put my gun in my pocket and wandered over to the passenger side of the truck. I laced two of my fingers around Chase's belt while he rummaged through the glove compartment to find the flashlight. After finding it, he grabbed hold of my belt.

"Come on Killer," I said, tugging on him.

Killer jumped out and took off at a full run.

"Killer! Killer! Get back here! Damn!" He was gone.

"He'll be alright. If we're lucky he'll find Max."

"Sure he will," I said sarcastically, "if he finds Max I'll cook him a steak."

Chapter Eight

We kept our eyes directed towards the road to avoid the snow blowing in our faces, and focused on paying attention to where we stepped. Chase moved the flashlight back and forth over the treacherous terrain, keeping us from veering off the road or breaking a leg. We trekked through the snow at a steady pace to stay warm.

"Did you see that?" I squinted through the snowflakes. I swore I glimpsed a flash of light ahead of us, but because I was freezing and my nerves vibrated like a wired outlet I wasn't sure. I pulled Chase closer to me. "Do you hear that?" I yelled, teeth rattling over the wind. "What is it?"

He came to an abrupt halt, concentrating hard on the sound. "I think it's a snowmobile. It's getting closer, maybe Killer found Max."

I pulled out my gun and gripped it as firmly as my frozen fingers would allow me, just in case the intruder wasn't Max. The metal hung heavy in my hand, like a huge icicle, made my palms tingle and numbed my fingers to the touch. I wasn't sure if I would be able to pull the trigger if I had to with my unfeeling hand.

Chase kept a tight grip on my belt loop, as we started

hoofing it up the road again the snowmobile suddenly appeared, barreling down on us, its light so blinding I couldn't see who was driving. We came to a halt, I aimed my gun at the snowmobile and held my breath.

I quickly lowered my gun. "It's Max and he's pissed."

"It's amazing how you know these things." Chase stated through chattering teeth.

Max passed us, turned around, and pulled up beside us, his lips pressed together in a thin line. I pictured him murdering us on the spot. "Put the gun away and climb on now," he growled.

Chase and I scrambled onto the snowmobile and Max took off at full speed causing Chase to quickly grab a hold of my waist. I did the same to Max.

"You're right, he's mad." Chase whispered in my ear as we held on for dear life.

Max cut the engine at the steps in front of my deck. Chase and I jumped off the snowmobile and ran into the house, straight for the fire, which thanks to Max was burning hot.

We planted ourselves by the fire to warm up, looked at each other and burst into giggles. I think it was a nervous reaction from the secret fear we both held inside on our trek home. We glanced at Killer, who was toasty warm already, and began to laugh harder. Max walked in with a dark scowl on his face. One look at him and we had to sit down, grabbing our sides from laughing so hard.

He sat down on the couch, patiently waiting for us to grow up again. It took a while for us to settled down. Once we did I held it together for a moment as I wiped the tears from my eyes. I made the mistake of glancing at up at Max.

His scowl deepened and I fell into the infectious laughter again, creating a domino effect on Chase.

Max got up and shook his head at us. "I'm brewing some fresh coffee; get it together before I get back."

We took a couple of deep breaths and I put my finger to my lips, letting Chase know not to say a word about today. Once we were calmer we started peeling off our wet clothes and shoes to dry in front of the fire. My last sock had a suction cup effect when I tugged it off my foot. I stood up in my shirt, and boxers, not quite sure if I was colder with my wet clothes on or off. Shivering, I ran upstairs to find some sweats for us. I hopped on one leg, trying to get my black fuzzy socks on when a giggle escaped my mouth. The image of Chase wearing my clothes skittered through my mind. He was taller than me and the sweats were going to look funny on him. I stifled the giggle, ran back downstairs and tossed the clothes to Chase.

Chase had just finished getting dressed when Max walked in with our coffee. Max took one look at Chase, slowly put down our mugs and began to laugh. "Chase that is not your style," he stated when he caught his breath. "Drink your coffee then go down to Roses and get some of your own clothes, check on the animals too while you're down there."

"Not a problem boss." Chase said, he took his time drinking his coffee.

Max silently held my gaze after Chase left. I lit a smoke and offered him one without breaking the eye contact. I wasn't about to let him intimidate me.

"I want your cell phone number and I want you to keep

85

your phone on you from now on," he finally said.

"You mean you don't have it. You're privy to everything else about me." I replied in a sarcastic tone.

He glared at me. "I need to be able to get in touch with you, at any time, night or day." Blowing out a breath he said more softly, "humor me; I'll make sure you have my number too."

I put out my smoke and stood to refill my coffee, in one motion Max swept me into his arms. He gazed longingly into my eyes, brushed his lips against mine, and then proceeded to kiss me so thoroughly I felt like I was being branded. Before I could think I was back on my feet, at arm's length.

Wow, little licks of flames shot through my veins from the kiss. I turned toward the kitchen and refilled my coffee. When I returned Max sat on the couch like nothing had happened.

I scratched Killer on the head. "I owe you a steak Killer." I was too full of red hot energy to sit back down, so I lit another smoke and pretended to warm myself in front of the fire. *Okay,* I was burning up from Max's kiss and wanted to pace, but I didn't want him to realize the affect he had on me.

"Are you staying tonight?"

"Yes, and I'll be sleeping with you."

Great, that's exactly what I needed right now.

"I'm going to go make sure Chase is in for the night," he said, rising, "we'll sit down and talk in the morning."

I watched him leave and paced around for a while reliving the kiss, before trudging up to my bedroom. I put on the extra long shirt I bought for when Max slept over and crawled into bed. I wasn't sure I'd be able to sleep, but apparently the day had caught up with me. I was out in no time.

I rolled over in bed, a constant tap, tap, tap, continued to invade my sleep. I groggily opened my eyes, the sun was up. Ugh, my eyes blearily searched for the clock, 10 am, it was about time I slept in. I started to cover my head with my pillow, I could sleep for at least one more hour. The tap, tap, penetrated my brain, unintentionally I focused on the sound.

"So much for sleeping in," I mumbled as I got up and pulled on some thick clothes.

"Good morning." Max said when I walked into the office. "This wouldn't happen to be what you and Chase were doing yesterday, would it?" He asked, showing me an on-line article, while tapping a pencil on the desk.

I avoided his question and glanced at the headlines, *"Mystery Couple Donate Food to Charities."* A blurry picture of Chase and I dropping food into a priests arms was placed on the left side of the article. The shelter must have had cameras above the door, uninterested I pretended to read the article.

"Chase said you only went down for zombie movies and lunch. He said you needed to get out of the house."

"I couldn't stay here any longer with what we found outside and stop doing that." I said, pointing at the pencil. "It's annoying."

He grinned and resumed bouncing the pencil off the desk. "I don't blame you Montana, but you did tell me you would be in for a couple of days. That's one of the reasons

87

I didn't come back right away, you're safe in the house with Chase."

"We needed to get out for a while," I sighed, "I'm going downstairs for coffee."

"Killer, let's get some fresh air." I called, tugging on my jacket. I had my first cup of brew, gun, and dog, I was ready.

I peered out the front door, didn't find any surprises, so Killer and I stepped out. At least 2 ft. of snow covered the ground. The sun shined brilliantly in the horizon, making the white sparkle with beautiful rainbow colors, blinding me at the same time. I checked my pockets for my sunglasses and smiled when I found them.

Either Max or Chase had already shoveled the deck, and my truck was in the driveway along with what must be Max's truck. It was a black Ford Ranger 4x4 super cab with a roll bar and auxiliary lights. Sweet.

I leaned on the deck, dreaming of driving Max's truck when pin pricks began crawling up my skin. I took a sip of coffee, willed myself not to run back into the house and ignored the watchful gaze. Pure hatred emanated from the woods. I didn't have to turn around to know Max was standing behind me. He closed the distance between us and rested his hands lightly on my hips. The blind hatred became absolutely lethal when Max touched me.

"Can you tell me where he is?"

"Take your hands off me and let's go inside." I whispered.

He dropped his hands from my hips as I whistled for Killer. Squaring my shoulders I walked back inside like everything was right with the world. As soon as Max shut the door I spun around and grabbed his upper arm.

"It wanted to kill you! Did you not feel the hatred? When you touched me, I swore it wanted to kill you!"

"Calm down Montana." He picked me up, planted me on the couch, sat down next to me, and lit a smoke. I immediately snagged the cigarette away from him. "I'm not a sensitive like you."

"Watch your back Max, whatever is out there despises you."

"*It's* actually a he. Can you tell me anything else?"

"No, every time I believe I've pinned down *his* location I sense *him* in a different direction, *he* must move fast." I replied sarcastically.

Max raised his eyebrows.

"I want to talk about this more, but I need a shower. I can still feel his residual hatred flowing through me. Are you staying?"

"Yes, I'll be here when you're done." He rose at the same time I did, enveloped me in his embrace, and held me tightly. I wriggled out of his grip. He raised my hand to his mouth and kissed it, tempting me to drag him up to the shower with me. *Damn he was distracting.* I left him standing there instead.

I finished with my shower, took my amulet off the bathroom counter and put it around my neck, praying there was some kind of Mojo in it to protect me from the awful sensations I kept getting hit with. I dressed in some jeans, a thick sweater, and applied a touch of makeup before descending the stairs, and wandering into the kitchen. Max stood next to the stove frying bacon. I gazed at the fluid

89

movements of his muscles as he flipped the meat and sliced through tomato's. I couldn't resist peeking over his shoulder to see what he was cooking, BLTs, yummy. I could get used to him hanging out in my kitchen. With a sly smile, he turned toward me. I backtracked.

"When is Chase coming back over?" I asked, sticking my head in the fridge and pulling out Rose's rosemary bundles.

"I sent him shopping; he'll be back later this afternoon. What is that?" He pulled the bundles out of the bags.

"This is from Rose, it's supposed to provide protection."

"Rosemary?" He said, chuckling.

"I'm going to hang it outside, maybe it will keep that thing off my porch."

He laughed. "I'll go with you after we eat."

I also pulled out a steak for my knight in shining armor, after all, Killer did have something to do with Max coming to rescue us. I sat down to count the bundles of rosemary. Rose had made up ten for me, now if only they would magically keep the psycho creature and his nests away. I wasn't too optimistic about it, but anything at this point was worth a try.

"What's going on?" I asked after chewing down a big bite of bacon, lettuce, and tomato deliciousness.

"It's classified, so I can't tell you much until I get the proper authorization. I'm working on it right now, since your life is in danger."

"What can you tell me?"

"*That* thing is a male and he seems highly interested in you, which isn't his normal behavior, animals can't sense him, and he's hard to see."

"I already know these things, tell me something new."
Why couldn't I get some straight answers out of him?
Screw classified!

Max let out I sigh, contemplating what to tell me. "I've
been tracking him for quite a while. I need to capture and
return him, hopefully alive. Unfortunately, you moving up
here has made my life more difficult. He's taking extra
precautions to cover up his tracks now." His face hardened
as he raked his gaze over me. "He has a high intelligence
level and is brutally dangerous when he feels threatened.
Remember that."

"And?"

"Don't give me any grief Montana. You may not be
intimidated by me, but you'd better be intimidated by him,
he's very dangerous."

Max was wrong, he did intimidate me and that thing
did scare me.

"So what do we do now?"

"You're coming to my house so I can make some calls.
Speaking of calls, I put my number in your cell phone this
morning and I now have yours in mine. Remember that."

"Okay."

Max's eyes became intense and his lips curved up in a
semi smile, "Just like that? I thought you didn't like me and
would fight me to the end." He said purring.

"Cut it out Max. I don't want to see you dead."

"So you do like me?"

"Maybe," I sighed under my breath. I stood and
reached for the rosemary, Max cornered me, swung me into
his arms and lightly brushed his lips across my face. My

91

pulse quickened as his eyes fixed on mine; his lips covered mine, softly, but possessively. The kiss seemed to go on forever, sending little electrical bolts through my body, growing into an intense longing. I was about ready to have my way with him when he reluctantly drew back.

"Let's get this done," his voice grumbled in a hoarse whisper. A strong scent of rosemary wafted up into the air from Max almost crushing tender herbs in his fist.

My heart slammed in my chest, my legs were weak, I opened my mouth to speak, but no words would come out. My feet seemed to grow roots into the floor. A kiss had never had that affect on me before and it unraveled my very being. Yes, he intimidated me.

Max put his hand on my back, pushing me gently toward the door while keeping some distance between us at the same time.

I slid into my boots without bothering to lace them, put on my jacket, and checked my gun. Max handed me my smokes and we went out to hang the rosemary, making Killer join us.

"He doesn't like the snow." I said with a slight grin. My heart was slowly coming back down to the "normal" range and my head was starting to clear. I found Killer's attempt to tiptoe through the white fluff amusing, even though he was failing miserably. Max glanced at Killer as he began to hang the rosemary.

"How many do you want to hang?"

"Just two, one by the front door and one by the back door."

Done with the first bundle, Max grabbed my wrist and hauled me over to the back door to hang the second bundle, then hauled me to the front door again to let Killer inside.

"You're being a little dramatic aren't you?" I rubbed my wrist. I wished he would stop touching me. I couldn't think clearly when he did and I needed to think clearly.

"I don't want you out of my sight right now."

"He isn't here right now."

"Doesn't matter."

We locked up and climbed onto his snowmobile.

"Hold on tight," He said revving the engine and taking off.

"Men and their toys." I mumbled to myself, enjoying the wind in my hair and the feel of Max's body against mine.

Chapter Nine

I was right; we crossed over the bridge and cruised onto his property. I surveyed the land, trees, and rocks, looking for my landmarks, trying to figure out where I'd gotten lost. His property was enormous. The land appeared different in the light of day with the snow covering the trees, and the sun sparkling on the snow. I didn't recognize anything.

Max slowed down when the trees became dense and we gradually wound our way in between them to a small clearing that led to his house. His house sat, or I should say, big cabin, sat inside the center of the clearing. I spotted a dirt road in my peripheral vision, or what I thought might be a dirt road. The snow covered most of the tread marks from his truck and smoothed out in the distance. A fortress of trees encompassed his cabin on all sides, making the area a hard place to find. I'd have to pay better attention to my surroundings on the way back home, just in case I needed to get back here on my own one day. As we coasted to a stop, I noticed an empty pen, but no wolves.

Max hopped off the snowmobile and followed my gaze. "They're roaming my property," he said. "I don't pen them up, but they do come back at night on their own and sleep in there."

"Why do you have them?"

"For protection, they don't let anything unwanted in."

My face paled. I'd been scouting Max's property with my dog and my horse while the wolves ran loose. *Did the wolves know I was here? Would they have attacked me if they knew?*

"Are you alright?"

"Sure."

"Don't worry, you're safe here."

"Rose said you're building a barn. Where is it?" I was pretty sure Max didn't have enough space to build a barn in the clearing.

"Umm…" A touch of guilt flashed in Max's eyes.

"You were planning on leaving your horse in my barn for the duration, weren't you?" Great, I'd already been stuck with Max before I moved up here.

He grinned and shrugged his shoulders.

"You do realize there was a good chance you wouldn't like me or want anything to do with me. I could have been fat, ugly, and mean."

"I did my research, so I knew you weren't fat and ugly. Mean is debatable."

I laughed, "You haven't seen mean Max."

Max's cabin stood two stories high, with a balcony on top and a deck on the bottom. The log posts were hand peeled. Through the windows vaulted ceilings with hanging ceiling fans gleamed in the afternoon sunlight. Of course, I only had a view of the back of the cabin, but it was magnificent and fit him well.

"I need to make some phone calls. Make yourself at

home."

We entered the cabin and he crossed the living room to what I assumed was his office. He closed the door behind him, leaving me standing there. *Were all men like that? Hot one second and cool the next?* Yet, another reason I preferred to stay single. I stayed rooted to my spot for a second, debating what I should do next. He just gave me the perfect opportunity to snoop around and I was trying to resist the temptation.

I pivoted in a circle. The downstairs was big with very little furniture, my kind of guy if I was looking for a guy. The kitchen was almost as big as the living room, with granite countertops, black appliances, and a huge butcher block placed in the center. Copper pots hung over it.

A huge fireplace, couch, and two chairs, graced the living room. I didn't find a TV or entertainment system. I walked to the back of the house where Max disappeared. I passed a full bath and an extra bedroom with a made up bed for company or Chase. I wasn't sure which, if Chase did live with Max he didn't own much. I tiptoed back out, passed the closed door, and searched for the stairs leading up to the second floor.

I stopped mid step and backtracked, I'd walked right by them and hadn't even seen them. Between the kitchen and hallway, a small alcove hid the stairway to the upstairs rooms. *Why hadn't I thought of that?*

The master bedroom and bath consumed the upstairs loft. The entertainment center stood to my right, against the entrance wall. Max's king size bed was placed on the back wall, across from the entertainment system. I sat on it for a moment, smoothed out the black down comforter, and surveyed the room. A second fireplace was built into the corner of the room, a couple of unused candles sat on the mantle. I stood up and searched around for some personal effects that might lead me to a clue as to who he was, but didn't find anything. *What exactly did he do? Was he a naturally secretive guy?*

I opened the doors across from the bed and found a massive walk in closet, on one side of the closet his clothes were hanging up. I flipped through them. I turned and rifled through his dresser drawers on the other side of the closet. A safe, small toolbox and guns hanging from pegs on the wall were neatly placed by the dresser. *Funny, I never recalled seeing him with a gun.* I eyeballed the 12 gauge and rubbed the meaty spot under my shoulder, remembering the fierce recoil, and bruise the 12 gauge gave me the last time I shot it. It took two weeks for the bruise to heal. I haven't picked one up since. Two semi-automatic rifles hung next to the 12 gauge and below them hung a 9 mm, a tranquilizer gun, and an empty slot. The guns spiked my curiosity. I opened the metal drawer under the guns and found boxes and boxes of ammo.

I continued to rummage through his possessions, as I wandered to the end of the closet I stumbled onto his master bath. I smiled, his bathroom was similar to mine, with granite counter tops, a separate shower, and tub, but without the Jacuzzi. We apparently had a lot in common when it came to decorating, less is better. I sauntered back out into the bedroom and ventured out to the balcony.

A hot tub rested in the corner of the balcony. I lifted the lid, warm steam rose up into the sky, enticing me to strip down and climb in. I could easily picture myself sitting in the hot tub, watching the stars light up the black sky, all the tension leaving my body. Max entered my dreamy picture, sitting next to me, naked. I quickly closed the lid and stepped over to the railing. I had to absolve myself of this problem quickly. Max was invading my space in my daydreams. That was a bad sign.

I lit a smoke and leaned on the railing. I tried to shake off the nagging disappointment of not finding out anything about Max, in his own house none-the-less. The air became still. The forest felt completely wrong. He was here. Adrenaline shot through my body, my heart raced, and yet numbness consumed me at the same time. *Where were the wolves?* I bent over the railing further and glanced around wildly. He appeared in my peripheral vision, in the pine trees below, just barely. I stared intently in that direction trying to get a lock on him.

"Montana?" Max asked, stepping onto the balcony.

I didn't answer; I was focused on trying to spot the thing again. If I wasn't mistaken he wore some kind of camouflage to blend into his surroundings.

"Montana!" Max wrapped his arms around my waist and drug me away from the railing.

The wolves began to howl, the pack raced into the clearing, sniffed the air, and took off at a dead run, disappearing into the trees.

Blood flooded my ears, I sagged into his arms. He half dragged me, half carried me into his bedroom and sat me on his bed, gently he brushed the hair out of my face. The soothing motion helped the shock wear off. He gazed at me with intense eyes. I yanked him forward and kissed him, then pushed him away and sprang off the bed. I rushed downstairs, gun drawn, with Max close on my heels.

"Montana stop!"

I threw open the door and skidded toward the snowmobile. I'd almost made it, but Max grabbed the back of my jacket and tugged. I lost my balance, my legs slid out in front of me and I landed flat on my butt. I sat there for a moment with my head in between my knees. The snow began soaking through my jeans; my whole body began to shake.

"Montana, are you all right?"

I sat up, tears streamed down my face. "I'm fine," I said, howling with laughter. I really needed to get better control of my nerves.

"Good. Get up so I can kill you."

That put me into a bigger fit of giggles as I stood up. "Whatever you need to do Max." I put my hands up by my head, still holding my gun.

Max glared at me. He moved forward and slung me over his shoulder so fast it made my head spin. He marched back inside the house.

"What the hell do you think you were doing?" He growled, carrying me back up the stairs. "Drop the gun on my bed."

I tossed the gun as he carried me into the bathroom and turned on the water in the shower.

I wrapped my arms tightly around his waist, "Don't you dare." He wrestled my arms loose, taking my jacket with him, and dumped me in the shower. I attempted to jump back out, but he pushed me back in.

"Stay there, you're freezing cold!"

I didn't feel cold until the warm water soaked through

my clothes.

"Strip down so I can put your clothes in the dryer."

I peeled my wet clothes off and threw them at him as hard as I could, getting his face and shirt wet. I knew I should have argued with him, but I was still in shock. I actually kind of got a glimpse of the "he creature." I had an idea what I was looking for now. My first reaction had me rooted to my spot on the balcony, but my second was to hunt it down and kill it. Max had stopped me, which now that I thought about it, didn't make any sense. We should have been out there chasing it down.

"No wonder you don't have a man in your life," he growled.

I stuck my tongue out at him and gave him the finger as he left the bathroom. The temptation to empty his shampoo and body soap down the drain overtook me, I was so mad. Instead of being childish and vindictive I turned off the water, plucked a towel off the rack, dried off, and put on his robe. I snuggled into it, marched back into his bedroom, avoiding him, and stood in front of the fire he'd just started.

I spun around and glared at him, seeing red. His arms were crossed in front of his chest and he glared right back at me.

"I am on vacation," I said very softly, my hands balled into fists. "I've had it with this thing that is out there! My plans were to spend the winter alone, reading, sitting by the fire, and doing what I wanted to do! Not playing nice with other people and not being locked in my own house. You told me I was safe here," my voice rose, "but that, that creature was hanging out in your pine trees, spying on me."

I took a deep breath. "You stopped me from finding it and killing it and you're mad at me? This is my vacation Max; this thing has got to go! Why the hell aren't we hunting it? It was right there!"

Max dropped his arms to his sides. "Damn, you're cute when you're mad."

I groaned. I should have expected him to change the subject. "Where are my clothes, I'm going home."

"Hold on Montana, your wet and your clothes aren't dry yet. Sit down and I'll get us some coffee." He disappeared down the stairs.

I wasn't ready to sit down, so I found a brush and brushed my hair with my head as close to the fire as I could get it. It wasn't a blow-dryer, but it helped a little.

When Max came back with our coffee I sat down. "I'm sorry about earlier, I had no idea he was here. As far as I know this is the first time he's ever been on my property. I heard the wolves scuffling around, searched the house for you, and then spotted you bent so far over the railing I thought you might fall. It scared and annoyed me at the same time." He grinned.

I imagined one of his wolves grinning at me like that and shuttered.

"Emotions I'm not used to having. You drive me crazy Montana."

"The feeling's mutual." I heaved out a sigh. "Any idea yet on why this thing wants me so bad?"

"No, and it's still classified. I'm done with my calls and Chase should be at your house soon. We'll head out in a few minutes."

He was evading my questions and probably lying. I

searched his eyes; he didn't want me hunting the thing down. "I need my clothes."

He snagged the coffee cup from my hand and killed the fire. "Follow me."

The laundry room was well placed under the stairs and hidden by a door.

"This is cool," I said, putting back on my semi-damp clothes. "Do you think your wolves might catch him?"

"No."

I wanted to ask him *why not?* But he'd probably just tell me I was cute again or something, so I let it drop.

We arrived back at my place without a problem. Max lent me his second snowmobile on the promise that I wouldn't take off. It was a hard promise to make, but I managed to keep myself in check.

"Hey, Chase. What's with all the food?" Chase had already unloaded the truck by the time we reached the house, and over-stuffed bags covered every inch of my kitchen counter.

Chase gave me a huge grin. "Ask Max."

I raised my eyebrow questionably at Max.

"Thanksgiving dinner, we're having it here. After tomorrow, I have to get back to work."

"Who's cooking?" I'm not big on cooking.

Max chuckled, "Chase and I."

I grinned, "Good."

After putting away the food I found two pizzas and placed them in the oven for dinner. When the timer beeped we took them into the living room and watched zombie movies until it was time for Chase to check on the animals.

Max went with him. I wasn't invited, of course.

I took Killer outside and lit a smoke. They hadn't invited him either and both of us were starting to pout. Everything seemed as it should be, so I leaned against the railing and examined the stars while listening to the wind blow through the trees. The night was cold, but at the same time, the chill was refreshing. I felt safe at this moment in time and decided to take advantage of it.

"You really shouldn't be out here by yourself," Max said softly, climbing up the stairs to stand beside me.

"All is right with the world and Killer is with me."

"He wouldn't be able to help you, though." Max slung his arm around my shoulder and held me close as we walked back inside.

"I'm going to bed," I slipped out of arms, away from him, and covered a yawn at the same time. Having him this close made me uneasy, both in a good way and in a bad way. I was confused. He drove me crazy even though I was insanely attracted to him. Not to mention everything that was happening overwhelmed me and my life didn't feel like my own anymore.

"I'm coming with you, I'll be up as soon as I check the locks."

Damn! I bounded up the stairs as soon as he turned his back and quickly changed into my nightshirt. I sat on the bed, putting on some purple fuzzy socks when Max emerged from my office.

"Nice socks," He said disappearing into my closet. He strode back out with black sweatpants on and sat on the bed next to me.

"Your clothes are in my closet?" *Why didn't I know*

that?

"My horse is in your barn, I'm here most of the time, it shouldn't surprise you that my clothes are in your closet."

I rolled my eyes at his arrogance. "Just as long as you remember not to get on my bad side, I'll be nice and keep a roof over both of your heads."

He grinned, rolling his eyes at me. "I'll remember, now climb under the covers with me."

He tucked us under the covers and pressed against me, hand resting on my waist. His breathing was even and he was solid. It was bad enough I had to keep my eyes averted from his beautifully, muscled, naked chest when he'd sat by me, now the intimacy from his closeness produced a rush of heat and desire that filled every part of my spirit. My heart went into overdrive.

"Relax Montana; I'm not going to bite. At least not tonight anyway, I'm exhausted."

I relaxed in degrees, vaguely remembering snuggling deeper into his arms until sleep took over.

Chapter Ten

I woke up to Max's stare. He'd just taken a shower and was standing over me wearing only a towel, small beads of water dripped from his hair and slid down his shoulders and chest. I bit the inside of my cheek to keep from drooling. My mouth twitched upward as my gaze wandered from his lips to his chest, tightly muscled stomach, narrow hips, muscular legs, and down to his feet. Concentrating hard not to let my gaze settle on any certain part of him I followed the same trail back up to his eyes. *Wow.* The intensity of his eyes startled me. My pulse gave a quick kick in anticipation. He sat down on the bed and lightly stroked my face with the back of his knuckles. "You need to get up," his voice rough, "Chase will be here soon."

I balled my hands into fists. It was all I could do to keep from yanking him down on top of me. I waited until he sauntered into the closet before I left the warm confines of my bed, reminding myself again that I didn't want to travel down that road. I went straight to the bathroom, locked the door behind me, and blasted the cold water in the shower.

I located my phone, turned it on, and fluffed myself up

105

some. I'd just booted up my computer when noises of pots and pans banging around echoed up the staircase. My phone joined the cooking sounds with its ring. I followed the sound, answering before it went to voice mail. "Hi, Rose, Happy Thanksgiving."

"Montana it's so nice to hear your voice. I'm glad you answered." Rose said, sounding down.

"You don't sound very happy Rose."

"I'm a little homesick and I haven't heard from Bear yet."

"Have you talked to him at all since you've been gone?"

"Every day, up until today. You haven't seen him by any chance have you?"

"No, but I'm sure he'll call you soon. It could be he's having a rough morning or something, it did snow several feet up here."

"You're probably right. What are your plans for today?" She laughed. "Let me guess, absolutely nothing. You're going to sit in front of the fire and watch movies or read."

"I wish. Max and Chase decided it would be fun to have Thanksgiving Dinner here. It sounds like they're busy cooking right now."

Rose was silent for a moment. "I'm glad you finally meet Chase, he's a good guy. What's going on with Max? What is he doing there?"

"He likes me? I really don't know Rose."

"So you're not dating him or anything? Did you find out anything else about him?"

"No, and no."

"That's too bad on both counts, maybe I was wrong and he'd be good for you. I bet you can't intimidate him as easily as other guys."

If only, he'd be long gone by now.

"I don't know what you're talking about Rose, besides I'm pretty sure I'd drive him crazy. I'm sure he'd be much happier with a more docile female." I tried to picture it. It didn't work.

"You need a man in your life Montana."

Here we go again. "I don't. How is your family?" I changed the subject.

We talked about her family for a while and I promised her if Bear didn't call her I'd go search for him.

As soon as I hung up with Rose my mom called. She was heading out with a group of other gals to the casino, and free food. I wished her luck. I didn't mention Chase or Max to her, I knew if I did there would be tons of questions and I'd be on the phone for hours with her.

"Don't forget to turn your phone on Christmas Day." My mom hummed.

"I won't. Have fun."

I hit the end call button and stared at my phone a moment, half expecting it to ring again. When I was sure it wasn't going to I snuck downstairs, out the back door. I wanted some fresh air without a bodyguard.

The forest was peaceful, the sun was out, and the sky was blue. The day was perfect. I sat in a chair on the back deck. My phone rang.

"Hey sis, how's it going?"

"It's going fabulous, we're thinking about becoming pregnant again!"

"Congratulations. When's the big day?"

"Ooh, not until summer, I don't ever want to be

107

pregnant during the summer again! Were going to try for a winter or spring baby, hopefully, a boy."

"Speaking of child, how's my niece?"

"She's yanking on my pant leg right now, impatient to talk to you."

I laughed. "And how's my favorite husband."

"You know he loves it when you call him that." She giggled. "He's perfect, as always."

My sister's name is Zoë; she has blond hair, blue eyes, is taller than me, and is the exact opposite of me. She's outgoing and friendly to everyone, plus she's always well dressed and perky. Her husband Shawn is one of my most favorite people. He has black hair with a touch of gray on the sides, hazel eyes, and a great body from working construction. He loves my sister more than life itself. He would do anything for her and Charlie, my niece. If I was ever to have a relationship I would like one like theirs. That one reason alone ruled out Max by itself.

"Hold on sis, Charlie is going to die if she doesn't talk to you right now."

The phone banged around in my ear for a second, I felt Charlie's high energy buzz through the line before she said anything. "Hi, Charlie, how much sugar have you had today?"

"How did you know I was on the phone? You know mom and dad won't feed me sugar. Mr. Lopez says hi too."

Charlie is the big three, has black hair like her father, blue eyes like her mother, and is a rocket. She's friendly, outgoing, and talks a mile a minute.

I let her talk until she had to take a breath, then I quickly asked her "How's Mr. Lopez?" Mr. Lopez is her giant pet turtle, I think she tried to ride him once, but he wouldn't move fast enough for her.

"Mr. Lopez has gotten bigger, I swear. Well, I don't really swear, mom says it's bad to do that."

I smiled, Charlie was a hoot. While she was rambling on about Mr. Lopez Max stepped out on the back deck with his arms crossed over his chest and my smokes in one of his hands. I grabbed my smokes, lit one, and handed them back to Max. He lit his own while he stood there watching me as I listened to Charlie.

It seemed like an eternity before Zoë was able to wrench the phone out of her daughter's hand.

"Love you, Charlie, we'll talk again soon."

In the background, I heard Charlie calmly tell her mom she wasn't done talking to me.

Zoë was laughing when she spoke. "Shawn just rescued us, he's taking Charlie outside and wishes you a Happy Thanksgiving."

"Right back at him," I said smiling. He was an excellent father too.

We talked for what seemed like forever. I didn't say a word to Zoë about Chase or Max either, she would have interrogated me just like mom if had, and I wasn't in the mood to answer any questions. She, like mom, promised to call on Christmas Day with a, "please remember to turn on your phone."

Max gestured me back inside once I hit the end button. As soon as we stepped through the door he backed me up against the wall, hands braced on both sides of my head and kissed me fiercely.

"I've wanted to do that all morning," he breathed,

109

kissing me more softly. "It's safer to kiss you with clothes on right now." He moved to my throat, left a small trail of fire as he proceeded to kiss my neck, up to my ear. Goose bumps danced up my arms, hot shivers shot down my spine. I slid my fingers down his chest, taking my time, resting my hands on his hips. *Oh man, he felt so right.*

"Bear's here," I whispered in his ear, lightly pushing him away, saved by the bell. *What did my body not understand about the word no!* Had Bear not interrupted us I would have wound my hands into his hair and continued kissing him for the rest of the morning. It was getting harder to keep my distance from him. I was losing control over this situation and he wasn't helping.

Max dragged his hands through his hair, his breathing uneven. "That's becoming annoying."

I gave a shaky laugh. "I can't help it; it's a blessing and a curse." More of a blessing than a curse, I thought.

We both tried to shake off our desire as we ventured to the front door to let Bear in.

"Make sure to wait until he knocks, he doesn't know you can do this and I don't want him to," Max said, slowing down our pace.

Max didn't need to remind me, most people didn't know I was a sensitive. I preferred to keep it that way. I waved to Chase on the way to the front door, patiently waited for Bear to knock, then gave it another minute before I answered.

"Hey Bear, what a nice surprise, come on in."

Max grasped my hand tightly. I couldn't shake it loose, so I had to step to the side to let everyone in.

"Montana, Max." Bear stomped his feet, shaking some

of the snow off his boots while eying Max's hand in mine at the same time.

"I hope you don't mind, my son Tree and I wanted to drop off some pumpkin pies for you and ended up picking up some hitchhikers on the drive over. This is my son Joshua; just call him Tree, Alexis, and Trina."

They all crowded into my kitchen. "Oh man, it smells so good in here," Alexis exclaimed, breathing in the scents of food from Chase's cooking.

Bear came up behind me and tugged on my shirt, causing Max to tighten his grip on my hand even more.

"Can I use your phone to call Rose? It's been a hectic morning," he blushed, "I forgot mine at home."

"Sure," I dug it out of my back pocket, "use the solarium."

"Okay, Max, what gives?" I whispered, holding our hands up while marching towards the fireplace.

"I want you by my side. There's nothing wrong with that."

"Hmm, now tell me the truth. I promise I won't run away or anything."

"Maybe not, but you sneak away every chance you get."

"I don't sneak, I walk."

Everyone moved into the living room, joining us. Interrupted again, this was getting very annoying.

"You have a great place Montana, and I haven't even seen the whole house." Alexis giggled as she spoke. "I hope you don't mind us barging in on you. Our car broke down close to town. Bear and Tree were nice enough to tow us to the nearest garage, before inviting us up here to drop off the pies. They said they could get us a room at the cute little bed and breakfast in town while our car is being fixed."

"It's not a problem. What's your destination?"

Max lightly brushed his fingers over my knuckles. I momentarily lost focus on the conversation. No wonder I was always sneaking out of the house.

Trina smiled. "We are on a sabbatical, so we've decided to drive wherever our heart desires."

"Where's that?"

Alexis smiled and giggled again. "The hot springs, we're going to camp there for a few days. I've heard it's beautiful."

"It is. I've seen several meteor showers at the springs. Keep your eyes open for them and shooting stars."

"Ooh, shooting stars," Trina said, her eyes lit up at the prospect.

Alexis laughed, "Were from L.A., so nature is a real adventure to us. We did a ton of reading on the subject before our vacation, hopefully, were prepared for anything that might happen."

I thought about the psycho-man creature out there. I really wanted to tell them to go somewhere else, but Max said everyone was safe, except me. I had to believe him or go insane worrying.

"Well if you run into any problems my casa is always open."

"Thank you, we'll remember that," they both said simultaneously and broke down into giggles.

"Look who I found," Bear said, coaxing Killer into the room. He flushed red as he handed me my phone. Good, he was able to talk to Rose.

Killer didn't quite make it to the fireplace before Trina and Alexis pounced on him.

"What's his name?" Trina cooed.

"Killer," Max, Chase, Bear and I replied at the same time.

"Ooh, you do look like a Killer." Trina said, rubbing his face while giving him a hug. "A Killer hunk of a dog," she giggled again.

I think Killer blushed.

When Chase rose to check on the food I took the opportunity to break free from Max. I followed Chase into the kitchen, put some fresh coffee onto brew, and poked around at the food. "How much do we have?"

Chase grabbed my hand, "Enough to feed everybody." He leaned into me, whispering into my ear. "Be nice to him Montana, he really likes you."

"What's going on in here?" Max grumbled, striding up to us.

Startled, we jumped away from each other.

"Is everything all right?" Max asked.

"Better than ever," I replied.

"You never answered my question."

"Chase and I were discussing dinner arrangements."

"It looked like he was going to kiss you," Max growled.

"Are you jealous?" I regretted saying it as soon as it came out of my mouth. Max glared at me. Chase gave me a dirty look before turning his back and walking out of the kitchen.

"I'm sorry Max, that was uncalled for. You just startled me when you came in. I swear there's nothing going on between me and Chase, but to be honest with you, I do like him a lot."

This time, I had to grab Max's hand to keep him from stomping out of the kitchen.

"If I was to have a younger brother it would be Chase." There was no use in starting a fight between them.

I watched the anger on Max's face subside. He tugged my hair and chuckled. A moan escaped my mouth as he slid his hand up the back of my neck and pulled me toward him. *Oh man, oh man, what was happening to me?*

To prove I still had some self-control I stuck my tongue out at him and dodged his embrace. I heard Max chuckle again.

"I need a break before the party gets started," I said as I bailed out onto the back deck with Max on my heels. "And I'm trying not to sneak out on you anymore."

I leaned against the railing, scoping out my property. "Where do you think he is? I haven't sensed him lately and I feel like I'm falling into a false sense of security."

"I think he's in its molting phase. That's why I'm leaving in the morning." He surveyed the landscape.

"He's shedding his skin? Does that mean he's growing?"

"No, he's adapting to the environment, to the snow."

"What are you saying? Does he change colors?"

"It's classified. I wish I could tell you more, but I've already said too much. He shouldn't be bothering you for the next couple of days, but please be careful anyway." Max held my gaze. "Chase will be staying here, regardless, to keep an eye on everything."

I caught his drift, he meant to keep an eye on me through Chase.

"Is it safe enough to go riding tomorrow? Lightning's probably getting restless."

"As long as you take Chase, I need to get back inside. I've neglected my duties long enough. Are we done out here?"

"Yeah, it's starting to get cold."

He reached out to me, changed his mind, and dropped his hand back to his side.

Chapter Eleven

Trina was of Asian descent, with long black flowing hair, big brown almond shaped eyes, and clear olive skin. And, of course, had a career as a model.

Alexis was Trina's personal makeup and hair artist. Her long rich curly brown hair with golden streaks and hazel eyes could drop any guy to his knees, along with the perfect tan. I could see both of them posing for the camera. They were both thin with long legs and very tone bodies.

The men were in the kitchen cooking, "us" girls were kicked back in front of the fire. Alexis eyed me for a second, jumped up and flew out the front door. She ran back into the house with a backpack slung over her shoulder.

"I have an absolutely fabulous idea," she grinned, pulling me up off the couch. "Where's your bedroom?"

I pointed her in the right direction.

"Come on," she tugged my arm and led the way. "This is such a wonderful house! We should think about buying something like this up here Trina."

Trina just smiled. She dumped out the contents of the backpack on my bed, sorted some items out, and placed them to the side.

Alexis stepped into the bathroom and started the water running in my Jacuzzi. She rematerialized at the bathroom entrance, holding her hand out, Trina handed her a bottle and she disappeared back into my bathroom. The scent of Patchouli and vanilla enveloped the upstairs loft.

"Okay Montana, were ready for you, get undressed."

The look I gave her made her giggle.

"You're in wonderful hands," Trina said.

"It's the least we can do for you for feeding us." Alexis grinned.

I glanced at the backpack and all the lotions and potions surrounding it.

"Alexis wouldn't part with any of this stuff when we left. I tried to tell her we wouldn't need it camping, but now I'm glad she brought it."

I started to undress. "Where do you want me?"

"In the Jacuzzi would be great."

The water smelled wonderful, so I slid into the tub. I was going to enjoy this. My world had been turned upside down recently, I deserved to get pampered.

Alexis applied thick greenish-brown goop on my face and neck while Alexis started brushing my hair, adding more goop to it.

"Why aren't you modeling Alexis?"

"I used too, but I couldn't stand the yelling and screaming that went with it. The dieting sucks too. I like to eat what I want when I want, besides my heart really is in the creating and making of masterpieces for the models to show off."

"She means makeup and hair," Trina said, "and since

117

when do you need to diet?"

"Models are my masterpieces when I'm done with them!" She said, exasperated.

I wanted to grin at that one, but the goop she'd plastered on my face was hardening.

"So tell me about that big hunk of a man down there," Trina sighed, "he's really into you."

I wanted to tell her she could have him, but the paste had dried and my facial muscles were tight.

"We're on a sabbatical from men," Alexis said, "but I would take on Chase in a heartbeat if we weren't. If you ever want to try the other side, let us know." She winked at me.

Both of them would definitely be my type, if my type was female. I wasn't at that point in my life and hopefully, never would be. I closed my eyes while I soaked until a timer went off somewhere.

"All right Montana, I hope you can hold your breath because we need you to rinse all this off." Alexis pushed me under the water.

Once I rinsed off the goop and was dry, Alexis sat me on the bed and started making me into a masterpiece.

"All done," She said, about ten minutes later, "I'm going downstairs to check on dinner, I'll be right back."

"This is Alexis product, what we used in the water." Trina handed me a bottle. "It's oil free, so you don't have to worry about shampooing your hair out after you use it. When you need more just call her."

"Can't I buy it on line?"

"No, we've been trying to market it, but haven't found any companies interested right now."

"Is there any side effects?"

"Not that we can tell. It's made only with all natural products and we've used it for years without any problems."

"Do you have a name for it?"

"Not yet, were having a hard time coming up with one because the product is so versatile. She made a scent free one we can use at the hot springs. It's really nice because it's water soluble and doesn't pollute the environment."

"Make sure you leave your information with me, Trina. I invest in small businesses for a living and if I like this product we might be able to work something out." I smiled. I liked them both.

Trina threw her arms around me in a tight hug and jumped up and down. "Thank You! I have got to tell Alexis!"

"Tell me what? Dinners ready, they're setting the table right now."

I yanked my clothes on. Trina raced over to Alexis, wrapped her arms around her in a huge hug, and swung her back and forth.

"I'll tell you later. It's wonderful news, you'll love it!"

We raced down the stairs to find coffee brewing, a fire burning, and tons of food on the table.

"This looks wonderful," I said, glancing at the boys. All four guys sat, staring at me.

"What's wrong?"

"Time to put your eyes back in their sockets boys," Alexis giggled. "Didn't you look in the mirror?" she whispered to me.

"No, I forgot."

"Go to the bathroom now." Alexis gave me a nudge.

I did as I was told and almost didn't recognize my reflection in the mirror. My hair was lightly highlighted, soft, and silky. My face glowed, and was soft and smooth. My skin felt like it did when I was a kid. I smiled, her product would definitely be worth investing in.

"Montana," Alexis said, poking her head into the bathroom. "Everyone's waiting for you."

I gave her a big hug. "Thanks." Now, at leas,t I would die beautiful if I died by the psycho creatures hands.

"Like I said, you're feeding us."

"Actually, the guys are feeding us; maybe you should take them upstairs."

Alexis giggled the whole way back to the table.

We ate ham with pineapple and brown sugar, sweet potatoes with marshmallows, green beans with almonds, homemade biscuits, cranberry sauce, and creamed onions, along with a salad straight from my garden.

I concentrated on the food, ignoring the guys glancing at me, and Max's blatant stare.

We finished off dinner with coffee and pumpkin pie, topped with real homemade whipped cream, in front of the fire. Killer had been given his own plate loaded up with dinner and pumpkin pie, which he ate while we were having dessert.

Killer finished his plate and joined us in front of the fire, receiving pets from Alexis and Trina before settling down. We were all   full, happy, and relaxed when this awful smell resonated from Killers direction. Killer smiled at us as the smell worsened. Everyone jumped up holding their noses closed and hurried back to the kitchen. Max and

I jerked our jackets off the hooks by the door, calling Killer outside, while Trina sprayed down the living room with her perfume.

"I think Killer ate too much," I said, laughing.

Max pressed himself against me, fingers rubbing up and down my sides. "Man, you're gorgeous," he dipped his face and breathed in my neck. "You smell so good," he whispered as he turned my face towards his, gently pressing his lips against mine. He abruptly stepped back and lit a smoke for me.

"You've got to stop doing that Max," or don't stop at all.

He gazed at me longingly until I turned my back on him to watch the moon rise over the mountains.

Killer managed to evacuate my house faster than I ever could have. The kitchen was clean again and after several hugs the gang piled into Bears truck and left. Chase packed up some leftovers for Roses house and soon after, Chase, Max, and Killer left to check on the animals. I immediately lit a smoke when they were gone and located the pine air freshener, spraying the entire downstairs. Killer was no longer allowed to eat vegetables or pumpkin, I though smiling, he was ripe tonight.

I was feigning sleep when Max climbed into bed. He pulled me against him, spooning me. The heat from his chest touching my back emanated through my nightshirt and my heart beat with anticipation. He wasn't wearing any clothes to bed tonight. His muscles sent small electrical pulses through my skin. I squeezed my eyes closed and tried to keep my breath even.

121

"Montana, I know you're awake," he lazily traced his fingertips over my belly button and up my stomach leaving my skin in flames under the shirt. His fingers lightly feathered down to my thigh and back up, creating little sparks of fire. He stopped at my waist for just a moment before sliding his hand under my shirt.

My breath caught in my throat. I couldn't take anymore. I clamped my hand over his before he reached his destination. He chuckled in my ear and started kissing my neck. I told him to stop in my mind, but couldn't get the words out of my mouth. My brain seemed to be at war with my body. My body won. I let go of his hand, rolled over, and kissed him, tracing my fingertips down and across his chest, causing his breath to catch in his throat.

"Remember Montana you belong to me," he said as the heat from his kisses rushed through my blood, and his hands set my body on fire.

Chapter Twelve

I woke up late the next morning with my bed empty and a small ache in my heart. I was an idiot; Max probably screwed up any other relationship I might have in the future. No one else could even begin to compare to him, at least not when it came to making love, because that's exactly what he did. Not just once, but all night long. He was insatiable. My lips felt swollen, my body felt bruised in a good way, muscles I didn't even know I had ached. I was in post sex heaven. For some reason, it pissed me off.

"Wake up sleeping beauty," Chase said as I opened my eyes. "You look like you had a wild night last night."

I sat up, fluffing my pillow. "You're the only sleeping beauty in this house, Chase."

He laughed, handing me coffee before he spilled it.

"I'm becoming spoiled," I took a sip.

"Max told me to let you sleep in, but not too long, just in case you still wanted to take Lightning out."

"Did he mention how long he might be gone?"

"No, if he catches that thing he could be gone for a while. If he picks up another job he could be gone for months," he frowned. "He did tell me to tell you if you need anything to call his cell, he's going to check it a couple times a day."

I was an idiot. Regardless of last night, I probably wouldn't see him again anyway. We both lived in different worlds. I liked to travel, he worked for the government. I liked my independence, he liked to invade my space. There was no room for a relationship, and not once had he ever mentioned having any kind of relationship with me. It was just sex. Wonderful sex, but just sex all the same.

"Horseback riding sounds wonderful; I'll be down in about thirty minutes."

Chase grinned wide. "Your clothes are at the foot of the bed," he said exiting the room.

With a sigh, I got out of bed, showered, found some warm clothes, got dressed, applied some makeup, and dried my hair. I picked up my backpack and put my notebook, camera, and smokes in it before I ambled downstairs.

"Ready?" I called to Chase as I searched for my gun. My mind kept circling back to Max when all I wanted to do was focus on anything else but him.

"Almost, Max left you a present. I'm putting it together right now. Come take a look."

"Have you seen my gun?" I marched into the kitchen, anger flashing in my eyes. Max was gone and I still felt like he was invading my space.

"Your gun is in your jacket pocket where you left it. What do you think?"

"I think both of you have to stop feeding me coffee," I growled. Max bought me a black espresso machine to match my black appliances.

Chase pressed the start button and gazed over at me.

"Sit down; we'll leave after we try this out."

"You're starting to sound like Max, Chase."

"Do you want to talk about it?"

I shook my head no.

"Max was really grumpy when he left this morning too. Is there something I need to know?"

"Nothing, sorry. How long are you watching over me?"

"Until he calls or comes back."

"Aren't you tired of it? I'm sure you have better things to do with your time."

"Actually, it's exciting. Besides, you're like the big sister I never had."

"Are you an only child?"

"Yep," he turned around to finish making our lattes, signaling the end of the discussion. He added a touch of vanilla and frothed some milk frowning, then smiling, then frowning again.

"I have no idea how to do this," he said, pouring hot flat milk into our espressos, and handing me one.

We both eyed the coffee, wondering if the milk was still good from so much heat. I took the plunge first, blew on my questionable latte and took a small sip.

"This is really good Chase, flat but good."

After our jolt of caffeine, I made sure my gun was loaded. We put on our jackets and headed down to the barn with Killer following us.

Killer pounced on Pumpkin giving her lots of dog kisses as soon as we opened the door. I watched Pumpkin flatten herself. Her ears laid back on her head and she gave Killer the evil eye.

"Pumpkin should be used to that by now," he sidestepped the animals. "It happens every time we bring Killer down here."

"If she lost a little weight she might be able to get away easier."

He chuckled, "That's not going to happen until she has her litter and maybe not even then. I think she's a naturally big boned cat."

"She's pregnant? How long have you known? Rose will be absolutely thrilled."

We stepped deeper into the barn. I wasn't surprised to see yet another horse in the stall next to Ace's empty one.

"Who does this horse belong to?"

The horse was brown with a white streak on its nose and was scrawny thin.

"She almost belongs to me. I'm renting to own her. I had the vet come in this morning and give her a general physical to make sure she is in good health, that's when I found out about Pumpkin." Chase said rubbing her neck. "She doesn't look like much right now, but she will be."

"What happened to her?"

"Her last owner was a mean S.O.B. and the people who adopted her can't afford to keep her. I've been making payments to them. She's almost paid off." He said, grimacing.

I mounted Lightning, called Killer, and rode out of the barn with Chase walking out behind us rubbing the horse's nose and talking to it lovingly.

"I hope you don't mind taking it easy today, she's still a little skittish."

"Not a problem."

126

He mounted her carefully, whispering in her ear to make sure she stayed calm.

"What's her name? Does Rose know about Pumpkin?"

"No name yet, I want to see how she behaves first. And no, I haven't had a chance to talk to Rose yet."

"You could name her Brownie or Bolt," I said as we rode towards the meadow.

We went through many more names for his horse, coming up with nothing that fit when we noticed the clouds rolling in.

"Time to go back, it's going to snow soon." Chase said as flurries started flying from the sky, the air became rapidly colder.

"Too late," I chuckled. We nudged the horses into a trot. The weather was another thing I loved about living up here. The sun could be shining without a cloud in the sky, or like right now with the clouds in the distance, and it could still be raining or snowing.

By the time we made it back to the barn at least two inches of snow covered us, and another two inches flurried around us when we finally trekked back up to my house.

With nothing else to do, I decided it would be fun to order toys, clothes, and presents for the kids for Christmas. I also considered buying Chase a Santa outfit.

We both agreed we would rent a car and deliver all of our goodies in the middle of the night, so we wouldn't be seen. After spending hours online we tried making lattes again. They came out somewhat better, if not a tad bit messier.

"Who needs to read directions," I told Chase, wiping the excess milk off the walls and counter tops. "We just

127

need practice."

We popped some popcorn then watched a zombie movie. The snow still created a white veil outside, and I was happy. Absolutely nothing bad had happened today, it was great.

I jumped out of bed and ran to the window, shrugging on my robe at the same time. I looked out to blue skies, sunshine, and a blanket of sparkling, white, snow everywhere. My deck was covered, I didn't think we would be able to get out of the house. Life was wonderful. I hurriedly got dressed in the warmest clothes I could find, ignoring the clothes Max had - probably- intentionally - left in my closet, and ran downstairs for my first latte.

"Hey," Chase said, poking the fire until the flames roared.

"Good morning! Coffee?"

"Yes, please."

"We really need to get you a bed; especially if you're going to be here awhile," I noted the pile of blankets still on the floor.

Chase glanced down at his makeshift bed. "Nah, I'm fine. Killer sleeps right up against me and we're in front of the fire. Did you know that Killer gets cold? He crawls under the blanket with me every night. You might want to consider getting him a doggie sweater or something."

I imagined Killer in a dog sweater, hit the start button on the espresso machine, and laughed. I would have to get him something in black since he was such a macho "hunk of a dog." I pictured him in pink and laughed harder.

"I'm serious Montana, he gets cold."

128

"How about a big, pink sweater?"

"Don't be mean, you'll hurt his feelings!"

"I was kidding Chase. It's just hard to believe my big, bad, dog needs outerwear."

Chase scratched Killers head. "She doesn't deserve you."

"I heard that," I brought out our flat lattes and rubbed Killer's ears.

"You know I love you, right?" Killer ignored me. "Fine, I'm putting on my snow boots and going outside to dig us out of here."

"You have your phone on you right?"

"No. I wasn't aware I needed it."

"I promised Max you would keep it on you at all times and forgot about it yesterday, so you need to go get it."

"Fine," I stormed up to my bedroom, turned it on, and checked my messages. Nothing. I stormed back downstairs and yanked my shoes on, reminding myself that I didn't want Max in my life.

"What did he do to make you so angry at him?"

"Nothing." *Max inserted himself into my life then walked out of my life!* I wanted to scream. I couldn't seem to keep my thoughts on anything else but Max.

I picked up a shovel. Yanking open the door I disturbed the natural order of things, causing a snow drift to enter the house. I tried to close the door, without success.

"Were going to have to shovel the snow back outside," Chase commented, gazing over at the mess I made.

I glared at the snow. "I'll shovel if you get the mop."

I gently removed the snow from my floor to avoid scratching it, then made my way outside. There had to be at least three feet of the white fluffy stuff on the ground. When I'd finally dug a walkway from the front door to the end of the stairs I stopped, looked around, and lit a smoke. Chase managed to coax Killer outside and was standing by me with his shovel when my phone rang.

"Are you going to answer it?"

"It's debatable," I pulled it out of my pocket and looked at the caller ID. I didn't recognize the number.

"Hello."

"Hey, Montana its Bear."

"How's it going, Bear?"

Chase glanced at me disappointed. I was pretty sure he hoped it was Max.

"Sounds good, I'll see you soon. Bear is coming to plow the driveway for us. If you take the left side I'll take the right, maybe we can get the deck cleaned off before he shows up."

We diligently plowed through the snow on the deck and barely finished when we heard the low rumble of the plow coming up the road. We stood there, freezing until he rounded the corner and I was able to get his attention. I signaled him to come inside when he was done; he waved back at us.

We were sitting by the fire with more coffee when Bear knocked.

"Come in."

He stomped off his boots before taking them off. "How do you like all this snow?" he said, walking to the fire. He peeled off his gloves and warmed his hands for a moment.

"I love it. It makes the fire even cozier."

Bear glanced around the house before looking at me.

"Max had to leave." I noticed the grin on his face he was trying to hide.

"Would you like an espresso?"

"Sure, but then I have to go plow more driveways."

"How much do I owe you for coming up here?"

"You have to give to our toy drive. That's the deal I make with all the folks."

"I'll be there."

"Also, do you mind if Tree and I visited tomorrow morning with our proposal? The bar and grill is on the winter schedule, twelve to eight. Is ten o'clock all right?"

"Sure," I said, watching Bear. I knew he wanted to ask about Max and was glad he didn't. "How are Rose and the girls doing?"

"Trina and Alexis are leaving up to the springs tomorrow, they've been keeping the bar a lively place since they've been here. I'll miss them, but I think Tree will miss them more. Rose is absolutely miserable. Both of us would rather her be here."

"Me too, I miss her."

"Pumpkin and I miss her too," Chase chimed in. "Tell her Pumpkin is pregnant and she's needed at home the next time you talk to her."

Bear smacked his hand on his thigh, booming with laughter. "Are you serious? No wonder the cat is so fat."

"I'm serious, but I can't tell you when she's due because she is fat and was adopted that way," Chase said.

"I'll let her know. It will give her something to think about while she's gone. Maybe it will even give her a good excuse to come home early." Bear pushed his empty cup aside, "I have to go, thanks for the coffee."

131

We said goodbye to Bear. I headed upstairs to check on my business dealings, grabbed my laptop and got comfortable on my bed. I noticed my gun sitting on the dresser, smacked myself on the forehead and reminded myself I needed to remember to carry it, even if everything was peaceful.

The rest of the day went smooth. When I finished with business I took the laptop downstairs and Chase and I surfed websites for outdoor wear for Killer. I couldn't motivate myself to do any research on the creature right now. It almost seemed like the whole thing was a bad dream and I was finally waking up.

After munching on Thanksgiving leftovers we headed down to the barn to walk the animals, then up to Roses to plow her deck. Another perfect day.

We hiked back up to my house, settling in with pumpkin pie and a movie before calling it a night. Once I was back upstairs I noticed I'd missed a call. Okay, so I wasn't used to having my gun or phone on me at all times. I dialed into my messages as I ran a bath, recognizing Max's voice.

"It's nice you remembered to turn your phone on Montana, but I need you to carry it around with you at all times." A flame ignited in my belly from listening to his sexy voice. "I was just checking in. I wanted to make sure you were all right and remind you if you need anything to give me a call. I will drop what I'm doing and come back."

I hit save and sunk into the nice hot water dreaming of Max. When my skin started to look like raisins I got out and snuggled into my bed.

Chapter Thirteen

I shook off the nightmare, opened my eyes, and realized the nightmare was happening in real time. Three big burly men, dressed in black, with black ski masks over their heads stood next to my bed. I blinked. *This is not a drill* the little voice inside my head told me. *Your gun is on the dresser. You have to get it right now.* I couldn't believe I let myself get into this situation. My gun should have been next to me on the table, or better yet, under my pillow. *Get a grip Montana, don't freak out, they haven't noticed you're awake, yet.* I glanced at them with half lidded eyes. The small sliver of the moon outside didn't shine enough light in my room to see what they were doing. But at the moment they weren't paying much attention to me, so I took a deep, quiet, breath and pounced out of bed with my arms swinging, going for my gun.

Halfway to the dresser, one of them grabbed me. He put his hand over my mouth so quickly it made my head spin. He clutched my waist, digging his fingers into my flesh, and tried to push me back onto the bed. I rounded on him the best I could and punched him hard in the ribs. Another guy yanked my wrists, getting a good grip, he pulled my arms away.

With my legs still free I started kicking at them wildly. As the two men wrangled me back onto the bed the third man wrestled for my legs. He was strong, but I was able to get that one good kick into his jaw, sending him flying into the dresser. I felt a pinprick, my body went limp immediately. They placed me back on my bed.

Okay, now it's time to freak out, my little voice said. I couldn't move. I was ready to freak out, my calmer side started writing down notes instead. I wanted to laugh. That damn nervous reaction again. Laughing was better than crying any day as far as I was concerned.

Mental note: all three wore black. They were definitely human. Not one of them had mumbled a word the entire time they were restraining me. They were professionals. My eyes became heavy. I tried to get any kind of description of them that I could, to no avail. Everything happened way to fast. I felt another pinprick as I nodded off.

My alarm clock kept beeping annoyingly. I opened my blurry eyes, found it and turned it off. I gazed at the ceiling for a while and wondered why my brain was so fuzzy. When my mind started to clear, bits and pieces of the night before flooded back to me in one quick rush. *Those men drugged me!*

I bolted out of bed, my head spun, my body felt like a ton of bricks weighed it down, and I became really nauseous. I dropped down to the floor, taking deeps breaths I crawled into the bathroom, barely making it to the toilet. I threw up. After my stomach emptied its contents I rested my head on the cool tile floor for a moment, letting the nausea pass.

Thoughts of Chase and Killer downstairs brought me back to reality. *Damn. I needed to make sure they were all right.* I laid there, rattled to my core, shaking all over, and terrified to stand back up. *What if I couldn't stomach moving? What if my head started spinning again? What if...?* Taking several deep breaths, I forced myself to focus. I couldn't, wouldn't think about the what ifs. So what if my muscles felt too heavy in my skin right now, I wouldn't let that stop me from checking out the situation, from checking on Chase and Killer.

Slowly, I crawled back into my bedroom on my hands and knees, passed the bed and headed towards the dresser. I glanced up; sunlight gleamed off my gun, all I needed to do was reach it. I hefted my arms up, put my hands on the edge of the dresser and lifted myself at the same time. Halfway there my head began to swim again. I dry-heaved a few times but kept going, taking deep breaths every step of the way. A million years later.., at least, that's what it seemed like, I held onto the dresser tightly, steadying myself.

Tears ran down my face from the effort I'd put into getting this far. And I wanted to cry more for the effort I knew it would take to get down to Chase and Killer. I wanted to crawl into a ball on the floor and forget everything. Instead, I looked up into the cracked mirror to make sure I hadn't been roughed up after I'd been knocked out. No visible bruises. I actually looked pretty good, I thought, smiling trough the tears. *That a girl, positive thinking.*

I imagined the guy I kicked, my smile grew, and I hoped he had a big bruise from it or better yet, a broken jaw. Maybe I broke the other guy's ribs too. I glanced down at my foot; my toes were swollen; slightly bruised. It was definitely worth it. I noticed the red hand prints on my arms when I picked up my gun and sighed, I could live with a few bruises. I checked my gun for bullets then focused on getting downstairs.

I stepped wobbly to the wall, pressed against it, and slid to the second-floor landing, taking small steps to the staircase. A bad sense of vertigo overcame me when I looked at the spiral staircase, my stomach curled. With no choice but to go down them, I closed my eyes tightly and slid down the wall onto my butt, then slid down the stairs. The vertigo passed when I sat firmly on the solarium floor. Taking another deep, shaky breath I crawled into the living room, staying low, gun ready.

The boys laid dead still under the blankets. I closed in on them, saw Killer panting, and scooted around him to check Chase. He was breathing fine and began to stir. I let out the breath I held, scanned his arms for pin pricks, and found one. They both must have been knocked out like me. I leaned back against the couch and stretched until I felt my muscles loosen up. I found one hole in Chase's arm and I had two. *What did it mean? What did those men stick in me that they didn't stick in Chase?* I glanced at them, it would probably be better if I let them wake up on their own. Without disturbing them I slowly stood, gaining some strength back I wobbled to the kitchen to make coffee.

The coffee was hot and burned my throat going down, but tasted amazing. Functioning better, I poured a second cup and tiptoed back upstairs. After a quick shower, I would go outside with my camera to see if the guys last night left any footprints or tire tracks. I'd also have to search the house to make sure they didn't take anything.

I wondered what these men wanted and kept circling back to the psycho roaming around my property. *Did I have information they needed? I didn't think so. Were they from a different agency? What did they want from me?* I had no idea what they were after, but my gut said this was about the psycho creature.

My arms started to shake as I got dressed. My body felt like I went on a drinking binge the night before. I plopped down on my bed and lit a smoke. A moan escaped my mouth, my head pounded, tears streamed down my cheeks, and my legs felt heavy again. I was starving and nauseous at the same time. I lit another smoke, wondering what the hell those men had done to me.

I finally thought my system was returning to normal when my legs started losing their heaviness and my head throbbed with a dull ache. That is until I became plagued with worry and concern. I lit another smoke. I needed to get it together. I expected Bear to drop by soon. I glanced at the clock, I still had a few hours. The sensations became stronger as Chase ran into the room with Killer behind him. I vaguely sensed Killers happiness at seeing me, but Chases emotions came crashing down on me like a ton of bricks.

"What happened? Are you alright?" Chase shook. I started shaking uncontrollably.

"You need to leave," I whispered, "go back downstairs and center yourself or something."

"What are you talking about? What's going on?"

137

Chase's agitation grew.

I groaned. "Your anxiety is killing me, it's too much to handle, please leave."

Chase stared at me for a moment, watching me shake and cry.

"I'm calling Max," he said, stepping into my office.

I could feel him trying to calm his nerves. It wasn't working.

"Please don't," I whispered, not sure if he heard me. Now he was worried and scared on top of being agitated.

I couldn't take anymore. I grabbed my smokes and closed myself off in the bathroom. I could barely hear him talking on the phone, his emotions weren't quite as intense anymore, but I was getting queasy again, and I had this crawling sensation under my skin. *This is what they had done to me. This is what they'd done to me!* I wanted to scream and not stop. Instead, I washed my face, screaming wouldn't do me any good. *Think positive. How could I be so rational about this? I must still be in shock. Okay, I would use this to my advantage, but I needed to get control over it now in order to do that. Then I needed to figure out how I would use this to my advantage.*

I applied some makeup while picturing a shield around me, to protect me from unwanted emotions. I brushed my hair, letting the smooth strokes calm my nerves until I was as ready as I ever would be to face Chase again.

Chase sat on my bed patiently, waiting for me, when I opened the bathroom door.

"How are you feeling?" I asked, working hard at keeping his scattered energy from overwhelming me.

"Calmer, but I'm more concerned about you," he

checked me out, "I called Max. He'll come back as soon as he gets the message."

I sat on the bed next to him, refusing to let go of my control. "You need to call him back and tell him it was a mistake. Tell him I had a nightmare or something."

"I can't do that. He'd kill me if something happened to you."

"You have to Chase. It's because of him this happened."

"I can't and I won't." He handed me the note. "This was left on the foot of your bed."

"HELP MAX," was all it said.

"Someone he works for did this to me," I whispered, crumpling the note, "but why?" The truth was too much for me to handle right now. "I don't want Max here." I didn't want to know how deep his emotions ran for me. I would if he came back, because of the stupid injection. I shook my head, worrying about his emotions should be the least of my concerns right now.

"I don't understand what was done to you, tell me."

I took a deep breath. "You know how I could always sense who was around if I'd met them? Well, I could also get a good sense of feelings and intentions too." I sighed, wanting to cry again. I wanted my nervous laugh back. I didn't feel like myself anymore. I didn't know if I ever would again. It didn't help that Chase's emotions were too intense for me to handle right now, and if Chase was this bad what would Max be like?

"They shot me up with some drug, now I can feel those emotions more. It's like they're 1,000 times stronger than before."

"What!?" Chase's face turned red, his anger building.
"Stay calm. Please."
Every muscle in my body tensed up, my anger rose, matching his. I felt like I was made of glass and at any moment would shatter. Then, all of a sudden, his anger subsided, making mine more manageable. I chuckled; I needed to learn that trick.

"I need to keep control over this and I need your help. Stay centered. Bear will be here soon. Let's go get some coffee and set some food out. Okay?" I stated, hoping my muscles would loosen up enough to move off the bed.

Chase whipped us up some lattes while I pulled food out of the refrigerator, placing it on some trays. After I finished the food preparations I put on my jacket and boots, craving fresh air. Chase's energy continued to yo-yo back and forth from anger, to concern, to wishing Max would show up. His confusion was getting on my last nerve and I felt a mental breakdown coming on. I wished I'd never moved here.

"I'm going outside to scout around," I told Chase, picking up my camera and gun.

"I should go with you."

"No! Stay here. I'm not going far, just walking around the house."

He began to freak out, not sure what he should do, he studied me for a moment.

"Okay," he replied defeated. "Don't get into any trouble."

I laughed; I was in trouble up to my eyeballs. Actually, I was in over my head.

"Chase, this isn't your fault," I said, staring him straight in the eyes. "Check your arm. You were knocked out just like me and Killer."

I braced myself and gave him a hug, jumping back within seconds. Jolts from his tension raced through my entire being from the contact I'd made, and it felt strange. *Was I ever going to be able to touch anyone again?* Chase was only a friend.

I mentally flashed back to the intense electrical charge of Max's touch and my skin pricked. He affected me too much already, without this little gift I received last night. No way would I ever let him touch me again. I would probably die of overload. I shook the thought from my head, one problem at a time.

"I'm sorry Chase," I said, hurrying through the door.

I lit another smoke after inhaling some fresh air. I was a wreck and torn. I wanted to hightail it out of here, leaving all of this behind me. I also wanted to go find that thing.

I plodded around the house, avoiding sinkholes in the snow, keeping an eye out for footprints, while I contemplated my next move. The only prints I found belonged to birds and raccoons. I stopped and listened, I could feel, really feel happiness and excitement coming from the surrounding wildlife. I took it all in, letting the tranquility balance me out and sooth my spirit while searching for any evidence those men might have left behind.

I rounded the side of the house to the driveway. No tracks here either. *What did they do walk on air? Or maybe they flew in through the window?* Ugh, how aggravating, to top it off I heard Bear driving up.

141

I ran back into the house, tossing my jacket on the peg. "Chase! I need you to stick around for the meeting. If I freak out make up some excuse and get me upstairs."

He nodded his head. "I thought you were going to bolt and leave me here."

"Me too, but I can't do that to you. We'll work this out." Hopefully, before Max arrived.

"They're coming up the front steps. Would you answer the door please?"

Bear and Tree arrived full of excitement. I wanted to run away. Instead, I clamped down on their emotions that were zinging through me and offered them some food and beverages. Once we had our plates full we sat down at the island and got down to business.

This was the worse meeting of my life. Sweat poured out of my skin, under my clothes, from the exertion of blocking their excitement, and from concentrating on what they were saying. I prayed sweat wouldn't start dripping from my face, dampness was already forming around my hairline. I fisted my hands under the table as I listened to what they had to say.

They wanted to set up a greenhouse with a small organic market where the locals could shop. The building they had in mind was located next door to the bar. They also knew of several people with chickens, which meant fresh eggs would be available.

The problem with living in the mountains was the growing season was too short and everyone had to leave town to buy their groceries, which meant smaller amounts of fresh fruits and vegetables, and bigger amounts of boxed staples. Not to mention gas prices were high and anything delivered up to the mountains cost more. Bear and Tree heard many complaints over the years and now felt they were in a position to do something about it. They wanted to find a few close farmers to buy the fruit and beef from. They already had the fresh eggs and chickens taken care of. Their voices faded in and out as I looked over their proposal. They continued to explain to me they had already talked to many of the locals.

"Everyone wants to back us on this. But most don't have the income to invest with us." Tree said.

I liked the idea, but wanted to see the property first. I considered Alexis product, maybe Bear would put up a shelf for it. We agreed I would keep the proposal overnight, reread it, and change anything I might feel needed changes.

"I would like to examine the property in the morning and then go over the proposal one more time if needed."

They got up to leave. I didn't need to spend much time on this. I knew they would do well. But I did need some time to get myself back together before going back out into the real world.

"Not a problem, this is going to take a while to get up and running, but it will benefit all of us." Bear reached out to shake my hand, making me cringe inside.

I avoided touching him. "I think so too." I wiped sweat off my brow and dropped my hands to my sides. "I think I might be coming down with something. I'll meet you in the morning."

"Stay in today and get better," Bear said as he and Tree left the house for work.

"Thank goodness that's over," I said to Chase as I watched them pull out of the driveway. "I have to go outside and cool off. Grab Killer and join me."

I stepped outside without my jacket, lighting another smoke.

"That's what, the sixth smoke you've had today?" Chase said, keeping some distance between us.

"I know," I leaned against the railing, rubbing my eyes. "I haven't smoked this much in years." I lifted my head up and glanced at the trees surrounding me. The snow sat heavy on the branches. The scenery looked like a winter wonderland. I wanted to be one of those trees right now, standing in the glory of nature with no worries and no sweat dripping off me. I put out my smoke. I really didn't need it.

"Will you help me do some research on the Internet today? I need to find a way to block this better." I laughed. "At this poin,t I don't care if its voodoo magic."

"I'll start right now. You're looking too pale and on edge. It's making my gut hurt. Come on Killer."

I took a few more deep breaths before heading back in to get on my laptop.

We spent the rest of the morning printing out different spells, meditations, and mantras. The afternoon trying all of them out. The meditations seemed to work the best. The mantras might have helped, but I couldn't seem to get the words out without giggling. After a lot of practice, I was able to block Chase better. I wasn't certain it would work on anyone else until I tested it out on Bear and Tree the next day. I wasn't looking forward to it.

By late afternoon our packages arrived. We were going through them when it occurred to me that we needed to take the gifts down tonight. I was only going to give Max a couple of days, if he didn't show I would take care of the problem myself. I'd planned on doing it before, but my mind was made up now.

"We need to take these down tonight."

"Do you really want to do that? I'm not sure your up to dealing with people right now." Chase said, glancing up at me. "You're going to leave aren't you?"

Was I that transparent? "I'm going to give Max a couple of days. If he doesn't show, then yes, I'm going hunting on my own. Right now let's separate all of this."

"I hope Max gets back soon then. I should call him again."

"Don't do that Chase, we should stop by a costume shop after we rent the car." I quickly changed the subject, "Your pick, Santa's, elves, trolls, whatever." At this point, I was rooting for the trolls.

He chuckled. "I'll have to think about it. Maybe we should use Max's truck instead of a rental, I'm not old enough to rent a car and I don't want you going inside."

"Do you know where the keys are?"

"I sure do."

"What about the wolves? Will we be safe from them?"

"They won't be a problem."

We separated everything, checked the weather, and hit the road, leaving Killer at home this time. Chase directed me to Max's driveway. It was nicely hidden, off the beaten path, behind a cluster of trees. His truck was in the driveway, covered in snow, his house dark and silent when we pulled up.

Chapter Fourteen

"Is it safe?" Chase said, gazing around at the enclosed forest.

"It is. The psycho could be 10 miles away and I'd probably know."

"Okay, I'll get the keys if you start brushing the truck off."

I got to work digging off the snow and barely made a dent when Chase came back with a wild grin on his face and a dangling key between his fingers. "I never believed I'd do this, but Max owes you one."

Yes, he did. I grinned as we finished removing the snow, packed everything in Max's Ford, along with some warm clothes, and the flashlight. I rechecked my gun. Call me paranoid, but I needed to make sure it was still loaded. My heart beat double time as I put the key in the ignition, then it started beating triple time. I stepped out of the truck until Chase got himself back under control.

"I hate this," He said when I turned over the ignition.

I blew out a breath. "Maybe it will wear off. Let's have some fun."

We made good time to the city. Max's truck drove

smooth and hugged the mountainous curves nicely. There wasn't nearly as much snow on the ground once we left the mountains. As soon as the road flattened out I hit the gas to see how fast the Ford would go. When we reached 100 mph Chase made me slow down to a more decent speed. I sighed, slowing down even more as we turned onto the freeway. After a couple of miles, we pulled into the parking lot of a costume store. I pulled into a space at the farthest point of the lot, with fewer vehicles surrounding us, and looked at Chase.

"Stay here, I'll be back in a few minutes," he jumped out of the truck and ran towards the store.

He jogged back to the truck about a half hour later with two bags in his hands.

"Sorry it took so long," he yelled over the noise of the radio.

The excess energy from people running in and out of the store had gotten to me. Most of the crowd lumbering around were frustrated and stressed, which amped up my anxiety level. I'd cranked the music up to try to block out other peoples stresses. Besides, Max had an awesome stereo system.

Chase tossed me a bag before turning his back to give me some privacy. It looked like I was going to be Mrs. Santa today. I changed, tightened the belt to hold up the pants then put on the wig and Santa hat. Chase lowered the volume on the radio and handed me his I-pod.

Mr. Santa grinned at me. "It might help some."

I giggled at Chase. The Santa outfit hung loosely around his sides and stomach. He needed to gain some weight or stuff a pillow under the costume to make it work.

I put the headphones in my ears but kept them at low volume. I still needed to hear what was going on around me. I was driving.

Darkness settled over us and cold seeped through the windows. We had our fingers crossed most of the city dwellers would be headed home for the night, giving me some kind of peace from the constant emotions bombarding me. Unfortunately, that wasn't the case, so we decided that if the boxes for donations were outside I'd pull up beside them and Chase would quickly drop off the toys. If not, I would park as far away from the building as I could.

By the time we'd made our third stop I'd burst out into a fit of giggles, had a bit of road rage, and then gone into massive depression.

I told Chase to put the rest of the toys in the next box we drove to. Every time I hit a red light the people in the car next to me would emanate their emotions right into me. After the last stop light out of town, I pulled over and let Chase drive. The kids in the car beside us were so high I caught a contact buzz and couldn't function anymore.

"Wow, check out the moo-oon," I sighed heavily as Chase drove down the highway.

Chase burst out laughing, which put me into a fit of giggles. He grinned, shaking his head as I giggled on and off most of the way home. I vaguely remember him talking to me and I'm still not sure what he said. I felt like I was coming out of a fog when he parked the truck at my front door.

"I don't ever want to do that again," I shook my head, trying to release the rest of the misty sensation stuck in my brain. The inside of my mouth felt like it had been packed with cotton. I needed something to drink badly. "Sorry, this time, wasn't as fun. Man, I have the munchies."

"Watching you stare at the moon in wonder all the way up here made it worth it. Maybe you should consider smoking some of the green stuff until this wears off, it seemed to relax you quite a bit."

"Not on your life, I don't understand how those kids were able to think, let alone drive."

I plucked my gun out of my purse, stepped out of the truck, and almost fell. "My legs are high. Is that possible?"

"I don't know, I've never touched the stuff myself." He helped steady me.

I hadn't either until tonight, and I still hadn't actually touched it. As soon as my legs moved of their own free will again I signaled Chase to stay behind me. I was probably being even more paranoid at this moment.

"We need to stick together tonight," I whispered as we stepped inside.

The house was clear, the back door still locked, so we went back outside with Killer. When we re-entered the house Killer's knee's were shaking from the cold.

"I'll start a fire if you make coffee."

Chase headed towards the fireplace, I detoured into the kitchen.

"I think I'm getting the hang of this thing." I grinned as I carried the lattes back into the living room, stopped in my tracks, and began to laugh so hard I spilled them all over the floor.

"Shh.., you're going to hurt his feelings." Chase glared up at me.

I glanced at Killer again and turned back to the kitchen

149

with the half empty cups, so much for my almost perfect lattes. I settled down and grabbed some paper towels, telling myself not to laugh as I headed back out to clean the mess I'd made. After I cleaned up I walked over to Killer and scratched him under the chin.

"You look so cute boy." I cooed.

"It was the only outfit I found that would fit him. And see he's not cold anymore."

"He's a green elf Chase," I tried to keep a straight face. "The body suit is alright, but the hat and booties are a little much, aren't they?"

"Nah, he looks good, besides, it will keep him warm. We can take him to Bears Christmas party like this, the kids will love it."

"You should wear the Santa suit if you take him dressed like an elf."

That way Killer won't be embarrassed, I kept to myself.

"I can do that," Chase grinned wide as he took off Killers hat and booties.

"I'm sleeping with you tonight, I'll go get my stuff and we'll crash down here."

Chase held his emotions low key. I knew he was keeping a tight rein on them. I sensed him pushing down his anxiety every time it began to surface and was grateful for it, but there was safety in numbers. I didn't want a repeat of the night before.

We checked the house again before getting comfortable on the floor with as much space between us as we could manage. Leaving the lights on we fell asleep.

Killer snored soundly under the covers between us when we stirred. Chase had his arm around Killers neck; I was stuck with Killer breathing hard in my face.

"Yuck," I mumbled, rolling onto my back, "I need to start brushing your teeth and maybe get you some scope or something." I took a couple breaths of clean air. "Stop laughing Chase. You ended up with the better part of the deal." I smiled, wishing I had the power to make Killer let out a good one in his direction.

"I'm going to search the house again then we'll take Killer out." Now I really was feeling too paranoid. I knew the house didn't need searching again, but I couldn't help doing it. What a nightmare.

Chase held out a cup of coffee for me when I wandered into the kitchen. I took the cup from him and called Killer. He wandered over to me, dressed in his elf costume again with his booties on, ready to go out for his morning constitutional. I stifled a laugh and yanked Chase out the door with us.

"I want you to come with me to meet Bear this morning. You can be my knight in shining armor if something happens."

"No problem."

I glanced at Chase. *Why couldn't I have fallen for him?* He was a great guy and really cute too. I gave him a quick hug, whistled for Killer then headed upstairs to my bedroom to get ready.

We both decided Max's truck was fun but needed to be returned to its rightful spot. I left a note for Max, letting him know we borrowed it and set it on the driver's seat while Chase put his key back. Jumping back into my truck

151

we drove into town and parked in front of Pops' Bar and Grill a few minutes early. I centered myself or tried to anyway. Chase squeezed my hand tightly.

"You wouldn't happen to have any of that green stuff on you?" I laughed nervously.

"Just remember Bear and Tree are easy compared to the city."

"Yeah right, let's get this over with."

Chase was right, they were easy compared to the city. Their energy bounced between excitement for their investment and apprehension the building was too small. I thought the building was perfect.

"Why don't you two stay for lunch? It's on the house." Tree said, putting his hand on my arm to steer me towards the bar.

Okay, the meeting went well until now. I clenched my teeth. Tree's touch zapped me of my remaining strength. All of his emotions raced through my body in seconds flat.

Chase saw my face turn pale and stepped in holding out his hand. "Thanks for the offer, but we really need to get going. The horses have to be exercised before it snows again."

Tree released my arm, shook Chase's hand, and glanced at the clouds in the sky. "It'll be snowing by tonight at the latest. The offer stands whenever you're ready."

Chapter Fifteen

This is absurd," I said as I searched the house yet again. I wasn't sure if I was being too paranoid or not.

"You're right," Chase replied from behind me. "I need a gun for just in case."

"Do you know how to use one?"

"Nope, but I can learn."

"Maybe we should get you a baseball bat until you do. All clear. Do you suppose I should do this every time we enter the house?"

"Probably, even though I'm pretty sure they accomplished what they intended to do."

"But I'm not out trying to find that thing."

"Not yet, anyway. I wish Max would show up."

We were out walking the horses when the first snowflakes began to fall.

"What if something really bad happens to you? Max needs to be there to protect you. Do you even have a plan?" Chase mumbled.

"I can take care of myself, and my plan is to take care

153

of this problem."

"How are you going to take care of the problem, you don't even know what's out there. Do you know the territory? You could get lost!"

I shrugged my shoulders as we walked the animals back to the barn.

"Would you please tone it down Chase," my anxiety levels shot up a few notches during his tirade.

"I'm sorry. I'm trying really hard not to freak out."

"It's all good. I don't want to freak out either, and I don't want to worry about something that hasn't happened yet." Although, every kind of scenario possible had been playing through my mind. Not all of them positive either.

When we arrived at Roses house I put my finger to my lips as I slowly opened the front door, gun in hand. Chase stood behind me, Killer sat waiting in his usual spot. Nothing had been disturbed, and as far as I could tell no one had set foot in her house either. I found a baseball bat in one of Roses closets and handed it to Chase as we locked up.

The snow was coming down faster by the time we clomped up my deck. After shaking off our jackets, stomping off our boots, and rechecking the house again we made ourselves comfortable in front of the fire.

The sun was setting when I finally got up to make us some grilled cheese sandwiches with tomato soup. I'd just put them on plates when my nerves became frazzled. I started shaking in fear.

"Chase, Alexis and Trina are here and they're scared. Let them in please."

My hands balled into fists as I worked hard on

composing myself when I heard pounding on the door. Chase opened it, the girls ran in knocking him out of the way, slamming the door closed and locking it behind them. They were shaking badly. It took all I had not to shake uncontrollably with them. Chase directed them to the fireplace, putting some distance between us.

"I'll get some blankets."

"Where's Montana?" Trina asked stuttering.

"She's in the kitchen," Chase handed them both a blanket, "deep breaths, in and out."

He waited until their breathing calmed before coming into the kitchen and wrapping his arms around me. "Are you all right?"

"Yeah, I think so." I followed his lead on exactly what he told Alexis and Trina, deep breaths, in and out. My nerves were shot. All of this was too much for me to handle.

"Grab those two cups of coffee and stay close."

I picked up the other two cups of coffee I recently made, attempting to calm my nerves by focusing on the espresso machine. I noticed my hands were still trembling badly.

Chase grabbed the cups from me; I balled my hands back into fists at my sides. He handed Alexis and Trina their coffee and we sat on the couch, Chase sitting so close to me he might as well have sat on my lap.

Trina and Alexis were sitting on the floor eying us.

They both said at the same time.

"Where's Max?"

The accusation in their eyes leapt out at me like I betrayed Max in some way with Chase staying here. I

155

wasn't about to explain the situation to them.

"Max had to leave."

"Tell us what happened," Chase said, changing the subject.

An icy chill shot down my back, my body vibrated, their apprehension rose a few more notches.

"We were up at the springs exploring," Trina said.

"It started to snow," Alexis chimed in. "And we were looking for a better place for our tents."

"We found a cave and decided it would be a great place to hold up until the weather passed," Trina interjected, glancing at Alexis.

Alexis shook her head. "We'd just moved all of our stuff into the cave and started a fire when we thought we heard something move."

"And something was watching us." Trina stuttered.

"We picked up our flashlights and guns, thinking we would search the cave better," Alexis shuttered. "You know, like maybe we were disturbing a bear or something."

"We took a few steps towards the back of the cave, and there was like green skin or something that looked like it all over the floor," Trina shivered, scooting closer to the fireplace.

"Anyway, the next thing we knew our fire was out." Alexis moved closer to Trina.

"And it was a good one too," Trina frowned. "We weren't alone and I don't think it was an animal. We snagged our backpacks and ran as fast as our legs would go. We thought we were lost. Then we saw your lights on and booked it down here."

"I hope you don't mind," Alexis said, letting out a sigh

and a full body shake at the same time. "I don't think it followed us, but it scared the hell out of us."

Yes! I knew where it was. A shiver crawled up my back. *I'd have to leave early. I would kill it then get on with my life.*

I let out a long silent breath through my teeth and tried not to grin.

"I don't mind at all. I'm just glad you didn't get lost in this storm. Both of you are welcome to stay here. Do you want to go back up to your camp in the morning for the rest of your stuff?"

They looked at each other. "No!" They both screeched with a nervous giggle.

"We have our backpacks, nothing else is valuable," Trina smirked.

"I have an idea," Chase said, nudging me. "We can put them up at Roses house. She has extra beds and they'd be comfortable. Do you think she would mind?"

That would work out really well for me.

"We'll call Bear in the morning for a tow. Is your car still up there?" Chase asked Alexis.

"Yes, it is," Alexis replied, glancing at Trina.

"We probably will need a tow with all this snow falling," Trina erupted in a nervous giggle. "I can't believe we couldn't find our car."

All three of them turned to me.

"Sure, but please be careful not to break anything. Roses house is eccentric."

Chase laughed. "That it is. Then it's settled. There's food down there, but I can whip you up something here if you're hungry."

"I could eat," Trina replied.

We stood up to head into the kitchen.

Crap! Not now! My heart nearly jumped out of my chest, my face paled.

Chase turned around when he realized I wasn't behind them and watched me walk backwards away from the living room. My arms were crossed in front of my chest, my nails dug into my sides.

"Help yourself," he said to the girls, "I'll be back in a minute."

I barely noticed Chase walk up to me. Max arrived, and he was furious.

I continued to walk backwards, staring at the front door when Max burst in. How he kept getting through my locked doors I had no idea.

He eyed me and Chase, and marched over to us, hands in fists, anger radiating out of his eyes. I stumbled, Chase caught me. I yanked out of his grasp and ran out the back door. I leaned on the deck railing and gulped some air. Chase stepped in front Max with his hands held up. I couldn't/ wouldn't take anymore of this tonight. My nerves were already wound up too tight because of Alexis and Trina.

"You have to calm down Max."

"Calm down," Max growled. "I've been trying to reach you since I got your message. Where the hell have you been?"

Max was pissed. His anger vibrated through me like a chainsaw, making my head throb and my stomach hurt. I stood frozen, watching them with tears streaming down my cheeks.

Max glared at Chase. "I need to talk to Montana. Let me through."

"No. Not until you calm down!" Chase spat.

Max pushed Chase aside and strode toward me. Chase swiveled, caught his balance, grabbed Max's arm, and spun him around.

"I'm not letting you near her until you get yourself under control."

Chase was getting extremely angry now. I wanted to help Chase, I really did. I wanted to step in and calm them both down, but my head felt like it was going to explode from the intense energy they were emanating.

I stumbled off the deck and threw up. When my stomach protested its emptiness I rose, wobbled down to the barn on rubbery legs, and crawled in-between some bales of hay. Holding my head, I cried until I fell asleep.

The next thing I knew Chase was picking me up and carrying me back to the house. He set me down by the fire and began to peel off my wet cloths.

"How do you feel?"

Mentally and physically exhausted. "Extremely hung over," I started to cry again.

He wrapped me in a blanket and held me until my tears dried up.

"So where is the big bully?"

He laughed. "Only you could bounce back that quickly. He's at Roses with the girls. As soon as he realized they were listening to everything he calmed down. We stepped outside and I explained what's been happening here. He went from mad, to surprisingly pale, to extremely worried, cursing the whole time." Chase laughed again. "It

159

would have made your head spin if you were here. We agreed he would get the girls settled while I found you and brought you home."

"I hate drama," I said, willing my strength back, so I could deal with Max.

"Max said he tried to get in touch with us. Where's your cell?"

"In my jacket pocket, but I haven't heard it ring at all."

He stood up to retrieve my phone. "It's dead," he laughed, "So is mine. We forgot to charge them with the excitement going on."

I giggled with him, it must be the stress.

"How's Alexis and Trina holding up? They must feel uncomfortable now."

"Nah, we just let them believe it was a lover's quarrel, they're rooting for Max winning the prize."

I laughed. My body solidified into lead weight and my brain was beginning to misfire from the stress.

I leaned heavily on the couch. "I have to get some sleep, Chase. I'll deal with Max in the morning if I can handle it."

"He promised me he would stay centered around you."

"Thanks for everything." I laid my head on my arms. I was on the verge of shutting down.

"I'll take you upstairs."

"No I will," Max said as he entered the living room.

Max pulled me into his arms and carried me upstairs. His heart beat against my chest and love surrounded me as he laid me down on the bed, pulling the covers over me.

Chapter Sixteen

When I stirred the next morning it was to total silence. I rolled over and spotted Max sleeping in a chair next to me. I watched him, remembering the love he emanated the night before. *Did I really pick up those emotions from him?* I couldn't be certain, last night was too hazy. It may have just been a dream.

I sighed, pushing the memory aside to dwell on later and glanced at the clock, still early, good. I wanted to get out of the house and up to the springs as soon as I could. I snuck out of bed and into my closet, put on several layers of clothes, and packed my backpack. Sleep had such amazing healing properties, I felt refreshed. I was on a mission. I peeked at Max to make sure he was still sleeping, then silently descended the stairs.

Chase and Killer were also asleep by the fireplace. I tiptoed by them and started the drip coffee machine, no need to wake them with the espresso machine. I slipped by them again, into the solarium, and glanced out the windows. Snow flurries, fog, and dark gray clouds lined the horizon. We were snowed in. So much for my mission, I grumbled. I remained stuck in the house with Max.

Sighing heavily I went back into the kitchen and

stashed my backpack. I poured some coffee into a mug and proceeded quietly to the back door with my boots, jacket, and other paraphernalia. I lightly tugged on the door, opening it without making any noise, and managed to get out without creating a landslide of snow. My feet sunk into the light fluffy stuff and disappeared. I stepped back, up against the wall, lit a smoke, and drank my coffee.

If I couldn't get out of my own house maybe the psycho-man thing couldn't get out of the cave. I thought about Max's snowmobiles and wondered how he got here. Most likely on Ace, but I walked to the front deck anyway to make sure. I'd definitely get out of here on one of those. No snowmobile in sight, and I might as well re-enter the house from the front door, Max was awake and getting more upset by the minute.

Bracing myself, I stomped my feet as I opened the door. "Good morning," I said, trying to remove some anxiety from the room before I stepped fully into the house.

The tension left the room faster than I thought it would, Max smiled at me.

"Told you," Chase said, yawning.

Chase raised his arms and arched his back, his phone started to ring. He grunted in mid-stretch before hitting the speaker on his phone, "Yeah."

"We're snowed in," Alexis chirped. "You should get dressed and come down here; we'll build a snowman and make snow angels. I'll even brew you up some hot chocolate mixed with coffee and make you breakfast."

Chase winked at me. They wanted me to be alone with Max and weren't being subtle about it.

"Let me call you back when I'm awake, then I'll stop

by."

I shook my head no behind Max's back as he turned around grinning at me. *Oh boy*, I knew where his thoughts were. He was standing there, wearing just his black sweats, looking totally sexy, and staring at me like I was breakfast.

"I'm going back outside to shovel the deck," I said, picking up a snow shovel. It took every bit of strength I had not to check out his half-naked, gorgeous body.

"Wait until I get dressed," Max coaxed, "I'll help you."

"I'd rather not."

The heat radiating from him started to envelop me or maybe it was the heat from me. I wasn't sure. All I knew was that I needed to get outside and cool off quick. I turned toward the door; he grabbed my wrist, sending a volt of intense hot lightning licking through my body. Before Max or Chase could stop it I dropped to the floor.

"Let go of her now." Chase's words echoed around me.

Max squatted beside me, attempting to collect me into his arms, when a blurry Chase pushed him away, picked me up, and put me on the couch.

"Get a cool wet cloth from the kitchen," Chase growled the order at Max

"Christ!" Max exclaimed. He hurried to kitchen and back, handing Chase a damp towel.

Chase pointed to the upstairs, motioning Max to leave while patting my face. I swatted his hand away, rested my head on his shoulder, and closed my eyes. Wow! And I thought Max was intense before. It was nothing compared to now.

163

"You're burning up Montana."

"It will pass." I thought about Max upstairs. Blowing out a breath I opened my eyes and spied him standing in the hallway watching us.

"Get dressed Chase and help us dig out, so you can go play with Alexis and Trina," I mumbled standing, still off balance.

"I'm not sure if I want to leave you here alone with him," he whispered in my ear, glancing in Max's direction.

"It's too late for that," I whispered back.

"Take care of her," Chase told Max as he went to change.

Max strode up to me lifting his hand as if to touch me. I stepped back. Max stopped short, dropping his hand back to his side. I could still feel little electrical pulses fluttering under my skin.

"Let's get to it," Max said, handing me a shovel. He took a step closer to me, brushed his lips across mine before realizing what he was doing, and stepped back. "I never meant for any of this to happen." His voice was rough.

Ignoring him I stepped outside. The snow should have melted by now, I thought, with all of the heat pouring off me. At least, I wished my body heat would melt the snow because it was piling up higher than before, and we hadn't even started shoveling yet.

I watched Max closely. He had secrets he wasn't willing to share with me. I knew for certain, I was being used. *Was he the one using me? Was it only his employers? Or both?* I didn't like being used. I wanted to be done with this mess.

"I know where it/he is or where he was last night. I want to go take care of this today."

Max raised his eyebrows then glanced behind my shoulder. Chase was attempting to pull Killer out the door. I hadn't even realized Chase opened the door, I'd been concentrating that hard on Max.

Killer wore his elf outfit and stood like a rock, on dry ground, not giving an inch. Chase repositioned himself, gave Killer a good yank, while talking nicely to him at the same time, and lost his footing. Sliding into Killer he landed flat on his back in the snow. Killer apparently thought Chase was playing a game, he wagged his tail and pounced on Chase's chest, licked Chase's face and sank them deeper into the snow.

I slid by Max, tugged on Killer, convinced him to get off of Chase, then began to dig Chase out as Trina and Alexis strode up to the deck laughing. I offered Chase my hand, planted my boots on the tips of his and pulled him up, out of the snow.

"Oh Killer, you look so adorable," Alexis crooned. "Come here boy."

Killer wagged his tail but stood his ground.

"He doesn't like snow much," Chase said grinning. He brushed off his clothes. "What's the plan?" He asked no one in particular.

"I'll be here for the duration," Max replied, eying me. "Shovel, then you can go do what you need to do."

"We'll help," Trina said, both her and Alexis clomped up the stairs with their cell phones out, "pictures first, though."

If Killer could blush he'd be a dark red color.

165

The girls posed beside Killer for pictures, knelt down, and proceeded to hug, kiss, and rub his face until he finally decided to brave the snow and wandered off the deck. Once the deck was clear Chase took off with the girls while Max and I stood at the railing watching the snow continue to fall. I sighed staring up at the clouds, not a hint of blue sky showed.

"Come on," Max said laying his hand on my back, pushing me toward the door.

I jerked his hand off me. "Stop touching me, Max." It had been frustrating enough dealing with the girls' high energy. His made my blood boil, literally. "It's time for you to find someone else to pick on."

"Ah, but I like you."

"Too much," I spun around, looking him square in the eyes. "You're going to make me spontaneously combust with all the heat you carry around."

He frowned. "Maybe there's a cure."

Yeah, right, if only I'd be that lucky. "Don't talk to those people about me ever again Max. I mean it! Cure or not."

"So what are you going do? Become an old spinster?"

"Or find the most boring guy on the planet." I glared at him. "I'm hoping it will wear off, eventually."

Max threw his arms around me, pulling me into his embrace before I had a chance to step back. He picked me up off my feet and kissed me fiercely, then set me down again.

"Not if I can help it," he growled.

My ears rang. My heart seemed like it was trying to escape out of my chest. I plopped down on the couch and

166

lit a smoke with shaking hands. Max plucked the cigarette out of my fingers and paced back and forth, brushing his hand through his hair. His agitation didn't help my overwrought nerves.

Was he using me? Or did he really care? I shook my head. I wasn't ready to trust him and definitely wasn't going to delve into his closed off emotions with this new gift of mine. Even though, I had a feeling I could if I really wanted to. I watched him pace until I was ready to scream. Instead of screaming, I settled for making us some espresso's and prayed he'd wear himself out before I returned. He stood in front of the fireplace when I handed him his coffee.

"Tell me where he is," Max said.

"Tell me what he is," I countered.

"Chase told me about the note you received. I've decided that I don't want you involved in this. Tell me where he is and I'll find him and take care of it."

I laughed ruefully. "I'm already involved, no thanks to your people. Besides your stuck here until it stops snowing, he might be long gone by then. You need me, Max."

"I'm not going to change my mind, Montana, you are staying here."

"Then how will you protect me?"

"I'll figure something out."

He was being pig-headed. I pushed him aside, stomped into the solarium, and sat by the window, watching the snow continue to fall. I did inventory in my mind on what I'd already placed in my backpack and what I still needed if I was to sneak out. After I made my mental list I snuggled into a ball and took a nap. I didn't need Max or Chase to take care of me. I was a big girl, I could take care of myself. When I woke it had stopped snowing and I was snuggled in bed with Max sleeping next to me.

Chapter Seventeen

I dug my fingernails into the palms of my hands to keep myself from touching Max. What I really wanted to do was brush my fingers down that glorious chest of his, nibble on his neck, and forget my problems. My temperature began to rise along with my heartbeat. I closed my eyes, rolled over, and silently crept out of bed. I unclenched my hands, blood formed in small crescent shaped moons on my palms from the bite of my nails.

I turned on the shower and stood under cold water. I needed to focus on that thing out there, not Max. After convincing myself I needed to ignore Max I toweled off, applied some makeup, dressed warmly, and snuck downstairs for coffee. Chase and Killer were nowhere to be found, more than likely they were at Roses house with the girls. Smiling I threw a few more things into my backpack, thinking now might be the perfect time to leave.

I sipped my coffee. No. I wouldn't get much of a head start and I'd be found, quartered, and probably duck taped to the wall. I debated checking on the horses but didn't want to get Max's back up. But seriously, this was my house, my property, and my horse. I should be able to do what I want, not sit and wait for him.

I sighed, feeling like a prisoner in my own home. I needed some air. I stepped outside and shoveled the rest of the snow off the deck, making sure to make as much noise as possible for Max's benefit. With that accomplished I went inside for a refill of coffee, then out to the back deck for a smoke.

My sixth sense kicked in the moment Max woke up and found my side of the bed empty. His eyes started to burn a hole in my back. I swiveled and waved up at the top window. I turned back around when he acknowledged me and stared out at my property.

"Do you sense anything?" Max asked from the back door.

"No, it's all clear."

I turned around to face him, trying not to notice he was in his sweatpants only, again, to no avail. He was doing it on purpose. My resolve melted away as my eyes roamed over his body. He hadn't shaved yet, and the day old stubble on his face was oh so sexy. My eyes skipped down to his rock hard stomach and trailed the line of black hair that stopped where his sweats rode low on his hips.

I licked my lips and forced my eyes to stop there. I glanced back up; his strong arms were crossed over his well defined, muscular chest. Heat radiated off him, tempting me to snuggle into his embrace. He cleared his throat. My eyes darted back up to his. He gazed at me so fiercely I started to blush. I darted around him and back inside before both of us fried my circuits, and busied myself starting a fire. Damn he was hot. I was thoroughly disgusted with myself. I had Max on the brain again. He wandered back inside a few minutes later. He watched me build the fire, then followed me into the kitchen.

"We should go out riding today," I said, pulling a protein drink out of the fridge.

"I don't want you leaving the house."

I yanked the tab open on the drink. "It's either going to be you or Chase that goes with me. Take your pick, because I'm not going to take no for an answer." I had a plan and I couldn't continue to get distracted, or let him get in the way.

"Fine, but I need some fuel first," he shook his head at my drink. "You should probably eat too."

"I'm not hungry, but if you go get dressed I'll cook up some breakfast."

He raised an eyebrow.

I couldn't focus on what I needed to do with him standing in my kitchen half naked, to top it off he was contemplating my cooking ability.

"Don't worry; I won't burn the food."

"I didn't say that."

"Yeah, but you were thinking it."

I stuck my head in the fridge and began to unload the breakfast items. When I closed the refrigerator door he was gone. I started the bacon frying and was whipping up some eggs when my internal radar picked up three more starving people and a dog hiking up to the house. Just what I needed, the universe was definitely working against me. I put more bacon in the frying pan, toast in the toaster, and began to make some spinach and cheese omelets.

"Oh man, it smells good in here," Trina said as they all piled through my front door.

Chase sidled up behind me and glanced over my shoulder. "I didn't know you could cook."

"I can. I just don't like to.

"I'll set the table."

"You might as well add two more, I hear the snowplow. Bear and Tree can join us."

I added more bacon and eggs, took a deep breath, then braced myself for the noise and chaos that was going to invade my space, and the possible mental breakdown that would follow.

Chase laid a hand on my shoulder, his calmness balanced me out, until Max came in. His jealousy was strong enough to break through, the noise rushed back at me.

"Here Max, you can take this out to the table," I said, clenching my teeth. I handed him the bacon, instead of chucking it at him. I have amazing self-control when I want to.

"I'm sorry," Max said as he came back into the kitchen and picked up the plate of omelets. "It bothers me that he can help you and I can't."

I reached up and slide my fingers down his cheek, the fire emanating off his skin ran down my fingertips and up my arm. Okay, maybe I had absolutely no self-control. I couldn't tell anymore.

"Its because there isn't any heat between me and Chase, Max."

Max lifted my fingers to his lips and kissed them one at a time, leaving a burning sensation on each one.

"We need to take out the food, everyone's starving," I whispered, breathless.

172

Max left the kitchen, leaving me to collect myself, yet again, before joining them.

I sat down at the table with Chase on one side of me and Max on the other. Chase kept his hand on my leg throughout breakfast, when no one was looking, to help keep me calm. Max avoided touching me altogether. Bear and Tree were explaining their business investment to Alexis and Trina while Killer waited patiently at the end of the table for his share. I gave Killer the toast I never touched, after refilling my coffee.

The constant battle with my lack of self-control around Max was driving me crazy, and now I had Alexis and Trina to worry about. *What was I thinking taking this on?* I was worth a ton of money. I could buy a new house and go to the best doctors for a cure. Of course, the doctors might think I was crazy too, but still, I didn't have to put myself through this. I pondered Rose, maybe she'd let me buy her a new house closer to Bear. And Chase, I'd really miss him, but he'd understand. I needed to keep my sanity. Max, well, I wasn't ready for whatever chemistry ricocheted between us anyway.

"Montana," Max said, gently touching my arm. "We can stay home if you want."

I shook the doubts from my mind. I had to do this for me, I wouldn't run away. I also didn't miss the fact Max called my house, home.

"No, I need some fresh air. Let me grab my stuff."

We walked down to the barn in silence, passing a huge snowman dressed in a blond wig with blue eyes, black eyeliner, rosy cheeks, and red lips. Either Alexis, Trina or

173

Chase sprayed gold buttons down the center of the snowman and thrown a purple scarf around its thick neck. Snow angel indentations surrounded the snowman. At least, they were having fun, I thought, dispiritedly.

The girls had been busy. A wooden plaque with the name Hershey's Kiss written in bold silver letters was mounted proudly in front of Chase's horses stall. A slight grin touched my lips at the name but quickly faded.

"Where do you want to ride?" Max asked, bringing his horse up next to mine.

"We'll stick to the meadow today."

He stayed close as we rode, watching me intently.

"What are you trying to accomplish?"

To use me as bait. I didn't tell Max that. It/he was out there somewhere. I could sense him, just barely. I hoped to draw him out of hiding by placing myself out in the open. He wasn't biting. At least not today.

"Nothing Max, the outdoors helps center me more than anything else I've done so far," I replied in a half truth.

"We should get you out a little more often then."

After we returned to my house I went upstairs, changed clothes, and found a kickboxing DVD. I stretched, ignoring Max, who sat on the couch watching me, and programmed the DVD for an hour workout.

By the time I finished exercising I knew what I needed to do next. Still ignoring Max, who hadn't moved from his spot, I headed upstairs for my computer, time to pull out my notes and do some more research. A shower tempted me, but hopefully, if I smelled bad enough Max wouldn't come near me.

I marched back downstairs to find Max working out.

Good, he wouldn't be bothering me for a little while, anyway. I detoured to the kitchen, grabbed a pot holder, the pot of coffee, some cream, and a coffee cup, before heading back upstairs. Settling on my bed with my coffee, laptop, and notes I got to work.

I slid out the handprint pictures from its folder. A shiver rolled through my blood from glancing at them and the memories from that morning came flooding back. With shaky hands, I laid them down on the bed, flipping them over so I couldn't see them anymore. Rubbing the goosebumps off my flesh I steadied myself and typed molting, quick, and blends into the background into the search engine on my laptop, coming up with a few hits. Mostly on birds and insects.

I thought about what the girls had said, they saw green skin, nothing about feathers. Birds and insects didn't seem right. I widened my search, typing in molting only. Birds, insects, crabs, tarantula's, snakes, lizards, turtles… The list was definitely larger.

I stood up to stretch while debating between tarantulas and lizards. Nothing else fit. Narrowing my search I typed in reptiles, molting, and camouflage, coming up with much more information than I cared to read about. I scanned through some of the sites before hitting on chameleons.

They weren't indigenous to the mountains, but they had a lot of similarities to the he/thing out there. They were normally found in trees and bushes, which might explain the lack of tracks around the area. They were uniquely adapted for climbing and visual hunting. They mainly ate insects, but the bigger ones also ate birds. This would explain the nests full of dead insects and birds that were

175

placed on my deck. They also shed their skin and changed colors to blend into the background.

I started to get excited. *What if that was what it was doing right now? What color would it become? It would have to be a pale color or maybe white to blend in with the snow. How big was it? Did it have a more human form than chameleon form or vise-versa?*

I scrolled back up through the article and reread the description of the Chameleon, concentrating on the information about its feet, then slowly went through the images until I found a couple of good quality prints. I picked up my pictures and examined them side by side.

My face turned pale, they weren't exactly the same, mine were a lot bigger, but they were too similar to each other to deny.

In the process of puzzling out the information, I sensed Max coming up the stairs. I quickly shoved my notes under the bed and closed out the web pages, except my email. I bent over my computer, looking busy when he plopped down next to me. He glanced over my shoulder.

"I've been catching up on work," I mumbled, hoping he would go away.

"You stole the coffee."

"There's an espresso machine in the kitchen."

He shrugged.

Ugh, what did it take to get rid of this man? I touched the coffee pot. "It's cold; I could go for a latte."

"How about you come downstairs with me and I'll make some for both of us."

"Okay." I closed out my e-mail. This would give me an excuse to get outside.

176

Even though I itched to get outside and see if the psycho-creature had moved in closer to my house, I was also interested in how to make a good latte. Chase and I still hadn't gotten it down. I watched closely as Max made the lattes. What can I say, I was spoiled and now that I had an espresso machine I needed to know how to use it.

Whipping the milk was all about the position of the wand to make perfect froth, plus a touch of vanilla and cinnamon. *Who knew?* Chase and I stuck the wand straight down into the milk, causing our lattes to be continually flat. I took a sip and decided that it was the best latte I've ever had.

"I'm going outside for some fresh air before I get back to work," I told Max as I put on my jacket and picked up my cup.

"I'll go with you." Max grabbed his jacket. "I thought you were on vacation, what's up with all of this work you've got going?"

"Bear, Tree, Alexis and Trina, what can I say, things happen."

"I knew about Bear and Tree's plans. I didn't know Alexis and Trina needed an investor."

"I'm looking into a product they have."

He laid his hand lightly on my back. "Why don't you leave for a week or two Montana? Chase would understand and I'm sure we could come up with a good excuse for everyone else."

"Are you trying to get rid of me?" I gave him my best smile.

"Yes, I am," he replied bluntly.

"I've considered it, but I'm not leaving. This is my

177

house, my property. I'm not going to be chased away.
Besides, if I leave this thing will too. I'm almost positive
I'm the only reason he's stayed here for this long." At least,
it seemed that way to me. "You want to catch it and I want
it caught. I'm staying."

He gazed at me intently. "I can't make you leave and I
wish you'd reconsider, but I think you may be right. As
long as you stay, he'll stay. It was worth a try." He lightly
kissed my cheek. "Hell, I can't blame him."

I left Max downstairs, went back to my office, pulled
out my notes, and searched over them for anything I might
have missed. After I scanned over them one last time I
stuffed them into a drawer and locked it.

*Could it be that some weird strain of Chameleon or
another animal was injected into a human?*

I began researching cloning on the Internet and soaked
up the information like a sponge.

Cloning animals continued to be the next big thing in
our generation. And now scientists are experimenting with
stem cells. Many things are genetically modified with a
special set of technologies that alter the genetic makeup of
organisms, such as animals and plants.

*Could this have been an everyday experiment that
went wrong?*

According to Max, this thing was highly dangerous.

*Could he be an experiment the government or some
other organization made for war?*

We already used guns, knives, bombs, weapons of
mass destruction, and much more. Not including biological
warfare.

178

Didn't we have enough ways to kill without creating new technology?

My mind wandered into conspiracy theory mode as I started to think about the secrets the government has covered up over the years. Not to mention the organizations that don't really exist.

I chuckled under my breath, a major cover up would be in order if the psycho/thing decided to do some massive damage while on the run.

The more I considered this new information I discovered, the less it surprised me. Most likely this creature was an experimental "Soldier." It made sense; he was quick, deadly, not easily seen, and animals couldn't sense him. What a scary theory. But then, I might be way off base, my imagination might be getting the better of me. The only way to find out would be to track it down myself.

I stepped into my closet and picked out some warm clothes. I stashed a knife and some extra bullets in the pockets of my jeans and hung everything up by some scarves. I wanted to be ready. I needed to be quick, quiet, and sneaky. Max wasn't invited on this outing. I chuckled lightly, Max wouldn't let me out of the house if he knew what I had planned.

I searched for my cell phone. Once I found it, I made sure it was fully charged. I placed it on the dresser and made a mental note not to forget it. I wasn't sure if I'd have a signal where I was going. Hell, I wasn't sure exactly where I was going, but it would be better to have it on me.

I rechecked everything before heading back downstairs for some food.

"Chase called. He's on his way over with some Ruben

179

Sandwiches from Bear's grill and Killer."

Drool formed in my mouth from the thought of Ruben's. "Sounds good. Is he staying?"

"No, he doesn't want the girls to disturb you and they're wiped out."

"Oh, okay," this needed to end soon, "anything on getting a cure for me?"

Max's glare made me wince.

"No, they're giving me the runaround, but I'm not going to stop trying."

"I bet it's an experimental drug and there's no cure."

"I hope your wrong."

"Chase is here. Do you mind getting the door?"

Chase's disappointment when Max opened the door unsettled me. Max scooped up the food and murmured something to Chase before closing the door again.

"Trina and Alexis are leaving in the morning and would like to cook breakfast for us as a thank you. Are you up for that?" Max asked as he set our food down.

"I'll have to be." Their timing was perfect.

We sat down at the kitchen table and dug in.

"You seem to be a million miles away. What are you thinking about?" Max stuffed the last bite of the Ruben in his mouth and picked up the trash.

I slowly lifted my head trying to conceal the light blush on my cheeks and looked into his eyes.

"Ah, I've thought about that a few times too."

"And that's all it will ever be," I sighed; especially if what I had planned worked, Max would hate me.

The heat from Max's gaze bore through me, making my body sizzle. His steel gray eyes were silver at this

180

moment. I could get lost in those eyes. I chuckled and grabbed my jacket and smokes. I'd probably heat up like this regardless of that awful shot. The longer I stayed around him the more attracted to him I became.

He followed me outside. "Anything?"

"No."

"So you're not going to deny it then?"

"Deny what?"

"That he's the reason you keep coming out here."

I shrugged my shoulders, keeping my back to him.

He closed the distance between us and wrapped his arms around me. It's a good thing I hadn't gotten around to putting my jacket on. I put up a mental shield, bracing myself for an on slot of emotions that never came. Max or I or both of us together were getting better at staying in control.

He bent down and whispered in my ear. "My next question is very important Montana. If he was even close to your property would you tell me?"

That was a question I wasn't sure how to answer. I wouldn't tell him, no, but I didn't want him to know that. So instead, I turned around in his arms and lightly kissed his lips, breaking his self-control. He kissed me back deeply and thoroughly, sending a blast of electrical currents through every nerve ending in my body. I started to sweat, then whimpered. Too much fire raged between us. Max must have realized it also. He kept his hands on my arms to steady me and he pulled back. We stared at each other for a moment, taking in big gulps of air as our hearts slowed down to a semi-normal beat.

"I'm not going to tell you I'm sorry Montana because

I'm not." His hands tightened into the flesh of my arms. "I want you and I will get a cure for you if I have to beat it out of them."

I swallowed hard, removed myself from his death grip, leaned back against the railing, and searched around for my smokes. I lit one and handed them to Max, he unclenched his fists, taking them from me. After tomorrow night, he would feel different. All I had to do was stay focused until then.

"You never answered my question. Would you tell me?"

"Maybe Max. He wants to kill you."

"He won't."

"How can you be so sure?"

He didn't answer; instead, he surveyed my property.

"He really isn't here, maybe he moved on to bigger, better pastures?"

"One could only hope," Max brushed the back of his hand over my cheek. "At least, you would be safe."

"Does that mean you'll be leaving soon?"

"I'll be here for a few more days. I want to make sure he's not coming back. I need you to tell me if he returns."

Chapter Eighteen

I snuggled in bed, listening to Max's even breathing, guilt assailed me. Reminding myself that everything would work out for the best this way I forced myself to go over the information I'd learned in my searches, instead of feeling guilty. I hoped some of the information I found was correct. If I was wrong about any of it I would be screwed. I turned the knowledge over in my head several times and pictured some of the scenarios that might happen. I wanted to be prepared for just about anything and everything when I went out tonight. I crawled out of bed and turned on the shower. It was still early, but I needed to start mentally preparing myself for our company now.

I let the hot water pour over me for what seemed like an eternity. Refreshed from the shower, I quickly got dressed and applied some makeup before heading downstairs for coffee and a smoke. Killer and I stood outside, enjoying the morning sun when Max joined us with an annoyed look on his face.

"You shouldn't be out here alone. I thought we went over that," he grumbled.

I smiled without answering. I was tired of not having

the freedom to wander as I pleased, of having to be protected every second of the day.

Max stepped up to me and cupped my chin. "I love it when you smile," he kissed my forehead, eyes, cheeks, and chin, before kissing me softly on the lips. Watching for my reaction he drew me closer, deepening the kiss. I intertwined my fingers through his hair, pulled him closer, and kissed him back with every ounce of passion I had. I suddenly needed him to know how I felt about him, without saying the words. This might be the last time we would be this close.

"We hate to interrupt." I vaguely heard Alexis say. The gang climbed up the steps onto the deck. "But we need to get out of dodge soon. The next storm is supposed to come in later tonight."

Killer's tail thumped against the back of my legs with excitement at seeing Chase and the girls. I dropped my arms down to my sides and grudgingly stepped out of Max's embrace, sidestepping Killer at the same time. It was probably better this way anyhow, my blood sizzled like red hot lava from the kiss. I would have melted onto the deck in another minute or so.

Chase, Alexis, and Trina grinned wide. I wanted them to disappear for a few more minutes. Max picked up on my animosity and quickly ushered the girls inside, leaving Chase and me alone.

"Does this mean it's worn off?" Chase asked.

"No!" I barked as an all consuming hate filled me. I massaged my temples, attempting to shake off the emotion and the fire that was still raging through my veins. I contemplated my surroundings. The hate filled emotion

184

didn't come from me. *Was the creature back?* I didn't get the chance to probe for him. Chase yanked me toward the back door, through it, and up the stairs to my bedroom.

"Come on Montana. We're going to work this out. Do you know what Max's plans are? Or if he's gotten any more information on the situation?"

"No, and no, but we need to make ourselves present downstairs." *Not.* "I wouldn't want the girls to think I'm playing both you and Max," I replied sarcastically.

Chase laughed, "I explained to the girls that we kind of adopted each other as a family, they believe me."

We sat on the bed for a few minutes while I collected myself. When I was ready we wandered downstairs to join the others. I gazed at Max as he started a fire, plastered a smile on my face, and tried to forget about him. My emotions seemed to be in a constant tug of war when it came to him. The anger I felt outside was finally dissipating, helping me to gain control over my scattered energy.

As soon as this was over I was planning on leaving. I wasn't sure where to yet, but it was definitely going to be someplace warm and far away.

"I'm going to go try my hand at the espresso machine again. Want some?" Chase asked.

Both Max and I nodded our heads. As Chase left the room Max tugged me to him, burying his face in my hair. I held onto him for a long heartbeat. Finally, I backed out of his arms before I passed out from heat overdose.

"Latte is served, and Alexis and Trina are going to attempt to make Huevos Rancheros. They've become addicted to green chili."

185

After breakfast, I wandered outside with Max and Killer.

"It's too bad we can't finish where we left off." Max leaned into me, brushing his hand through my hair.

"It is too bad." I stepped back, bracing myself against the hate filled air sizzling around me. That thing was out there watching us. I held back the urge to giggle, surprised I hadn't had a mental breakdown by now. It took all of my strength ignoring the psycho. I was ready to explode. I had to refrain from clenching my fists and screaming bloody murder.

I turned my thoughts to Max. It was interesting he couldn't sense the psycho, being a tracker, but I had to give him credit, his moves were light and swift. I didn't doubt he'd be able to track just about anything. If my senses weren't as acute as they were he would probably get a kick out of sneaking up on me. My problem was impatience. I couldn't wait any longer for him to track the thing down.

"Anything?"

I unclenched my jaw. "No."

I watched his steel gray eyes take in our surroundings before coming back to settle on me. His expression had become guarded as his gaze landed on my face, searching it for any signs I might be lying. I composed myself the best I could, put on my best poker face, and hoped he wouldn't read me. He was indecisive.

"The girls will be leaving soon and so will I. Chase will stay with you again. This time, keep your cell phone charged and on you at all times."

"When do you plan on leaving?"

"Depending on the weather I'll leave in the morning."

"We'll be getting more snow."

"Doesn't matter," he searched the area again. "We haven't had this much snow in years. I hope to use it to my advantage."

"I think he's done." I pointed my finger in Killers direction. I didn't want to think about Max leaving. Then I reminded myself I didn't want to think about him at all.

The change in the air as we wandered back inside was much better. Trina and Alexis were still charged with excitement, but the anger radiating from the creature loosened in intenseness.

"The kitchen is now spotless," Trina said as they both embraced me in a huge hug, picking me up off the floor. "We are out of here. Thank you for everything."

I looked at Chase and Max and mouthed help.

"What about me?" Chase asked, with his best pouty face.

The girls dropped me and ran to Chase, giving him a hug and more than a few kisses on his cheeks and neck. When they finally let go of Chase they kissed and hugged Killer before glancing at Max.

"It was so nice to meet you," Trina said. She stood there debating for a moment. She gave him a quick hug, Alexis followed her lead.

Chase walked them out to their car. I laughed, gave Max a quick hug, mimicking the girls. "You shouldn't be so intimidating." I batted my eyes, laughing harder.

Max chuckled at my antics. "I'm going to have Chase stay tonight."

My smile faded, and now there were two.

"I'm going to go take a nice long leisurely bath."

I stepped out of the tub, rummaged through my medicine cabinet until I found what I was looking for, slowly got dressed, and applied some makeup. After rechecking my backpack I grabbed a book and descended the stairs in search for a bottle of water and coffee.

"I didn't think you were going to grace us with your presence this afternoon. You've been upstairs for quite some time." Max said, cornering me by the coffee pot.

"This is my house."

"We need to talk."

"If you want to divulge any of your secrets I'm all ears."

"You know I can't tell you what's classified. I want to talk about this thing between us."

I held up my hand, interrupting him. "There can't be anything between us, not now and maybe not ever. Now move." I pushed through him, leaving him gaping after me, and settled myself in my favorite chair in front of the fire. I really needed to get him out of my system.

Chase kicked back on the couch with his eyes closed, feigning sleep. Max frowned at me, pulled out his laptop, and pretended to work, his thoughts conflicted. I was tired of picking up on other peoples thoughts. *Was this "gift" manifesting into something more? Would I be able to read people's minds soon?*

This had to end tonight. I lit a smoke and opening my book. I hurt Max with my comment, I didn't mean too, but the attraction was just too strong and physically exhausting.

Add to that the mental exhaustion and I'd probably be

able to sleep for a year.

My plans would be better for all of us, and I would have my house to myself again. I debated on telling Max what I knew, then dismissed it. He was way too big of a distraction to have around. I tried to concentrate on the words in my book, but couldn't, so I put it down and closed my eyes for a cat nap.

Chapter Nineteen

"I am so sorry," I said to Max as I kissed him on the cheek, "this has to be taken care of now. I can't live like this anymore." I laid a blanket over him and rechecked his pulse before kissing him on the lips.

Next I tucked a blanket over Chase and rechecked his pulse.

"At least, I know you'll forgive me." I kissed Chase on the cheek.

I rubbed Killers head and gave him a hug. "Take good care of them," I whispered, "I'll be back soon." I glanced at Max and Chase. "They won't even know I left tonight. I promise."

I sighed as I stood in the living room for a moment watching them. Determinedly I collected the coffee cups and washed them out. I grabbed a butcher knife, stuck it in my boot, and swung my backpack over my shoulder.

This is stupid crazy my brain screamed at me. *Who do you think you are, Wonder Woman? Yes,* I screamed back *I am Wonder Woman with Spidey senses.* I lit a smoke and closed my eyes for a second. With resolve, I yanked on my jacket, looked back over at Max and Chase, pulled out my gun, checked the chamber for bullets, and flipped the safety off before stepping out onto the deck. Cold dark air wrapped around me, a moment of dread overcame me. I shrugged it off, pointed my gun at the darkness, let down my barriers, and attempted to pinpoint my nemesis. I stood there for a moment, picturing what Wonder Woman would do and decided it didn't matter much since my Spidey sense wasn't going off. *Did this thing have an early bedtime or what?*

Exhaling, I crept off the deck, gun still pointed at the blackness of the night. I pulled the flashlight out of my pocket, turned it on and aimed it toward the ground, sweeping it back and forth, so I wouldn't trip over anything. I wandered around my property, avoiding the tree line, attempting to draw him out. Nothing. I walked a full circle and ended back at Rose's house where I climbed the deck and sat down.

I lit another smoke and glanced up at the bright twinkling stars. It was so cold out the stars shimmered. A star shot over the horizon, then another one, a small meteor shower lit up the inky blackness. The show was spectacular and calmed my wrecked nerves.

I debated on whether or not I should saddle up Lightning and head up to the caves. I promised Killer I would be back before Max and Chase woke up, but this was most likely the only chance I would have to take care of this my way. I didn't think I'd be able to stand not having my freedom for however long it took Max to hunt down and catch this thing. Lightning would get me up to the caves quicker than walking, but as dark as it was I wasn't sure how her footing would be. I blew out a breath. I

191

should have read up on horses, I really didn't know much about them.

When the meteor shower ended I stood up and stretched. I still didn't sense the psycho-creature. I had hoped to end this here on my property, close to my house, but it didn't look like that was going to happen.

I suppressed an icy shiver that crawled up my back. I had to do this for me. I would hike up there; the exercise would keep me warm. If I made good time and there was nothing to be found then I would make it back home with no-one the wiser. I straightened my shoulders, steadied my nerves, tightened my backpack, and set off at a good pace. Had I known what I was about to encounter I probably would have stayed home.

I'd studied the map and felt good about this journey and positive I wouldn't get lost. I stopped at the tree line, my adrenaline pumping. My Spidey sense still wasn't picking up anything so I took a deep breath and stepped into the forest. A whisper of a chill lightly caressed my neck when I found myself at the bridge separating my property from Max's. Hopefully, his wolves didn't leave his land.

I hiked through the woods, thinking about Max, and began to feel somewhat at ease when my Spidey senses rang the alarm. Pushing aside all thoughts of Max, and his wolves, I concentrated on the motility. My hyper-awareness registered a small blip at first, within seconds the blip shot off the radar. *Shit!* He was coming up on me fast, right in front of me. *What the hell was this thing?* I turned off my flashlight, focused all of my thoughts on him and raised my gun, aiming it into the blackness.

Should I stand my ground or should I run? I wasn't very far from the meadow; if I could draw him out there then I could shoot him and be done with it. The tree tops blanketed the stars, blackness ebbed out of the forest, and too many trees grew around me. I doubted I could hit my target where I stood. I slowly backed up, hoping I wouldn't trip over anything, or run into a tree. As soon as I sensed he was close enough I turned around and bolted through the shadows towards the meadow. He was right behind me and to the left when he yanked my backpack. I dropped my arms letting the backpack slide off my back, cornered to the right, and dived into some oak bushes, squatting down low.

Damn, he was too fast. I still hadn't seen what I was fighting. *Was this thing invisible or what?* I took some short deep breaths to calm the panic rising through me. *How could I fight something I couldn't even see?* I groaned under my breath, to top it off it was starting to snow. I cringed as the branches of the oaks began to rustle. He was right on top of me. *Double damn!* I needed to stand my ground here. I scooted back into the brush further and raised my gun.

Chapter Twenty

My head felt like a spike had been pushed through it, my body ached.

Why was I so uncomfortable?

I tried to move. Numbness weighed down my arms and legs, exhaustion threatened to pull me under. At least, warmth flowed through this place. I moaned and considered opening my eyes. A hint of light penetrated my eyelids. I considered glancing around at my surroundings. I kept my eyes closed, afraid if I opened them the light would be much brighter and pierce through my skull like a knife. I slipped back into an unconscious state.

The numbness in my arms and legs drove me back up from oblivion. My head still throbbed dully. I took my time peeking through my eyelashes, careful not to aggravate the obnoxious ache more.

I blinked a couple of times, trying to remember what happened. My memory was fuzzy and took a moment to penetrate my cloudy mind. I laid on my side staring at what looked like a cave wall. *Okay.* I closed my eyes. I knew who I was, which was a good sign. I brought the images of Rose, Chase, Max, Bear, Tree, Killer, and the girls into my vision and tried to piece the puzzle together. My memory wasn't totally gone, but my thoughts were too jumbled, and the throb in my head had slowly become a splitting headache.

I opened my eyes again. *Why was I in a cave? How did I get here?* If I figured that out everything should fall into place. I attempted to stretch out, my body wouldn't budge. *Great!* Steadily, I lifted my head off the dirt and rock covered floor and twisted my neck, glancing behind me.

My hands were tied behind my back with a rope, attached in a knot to more rope, attached to my feet. I thought I'd go insane from the numbness. I commanded my hands to move, sending prickly sensations into my fingertips as I glanced around. The fire behind me kept me warm and as far as I could tell, I was alone.

I glanced back at the fire. The most damage I could do was burn my flesh. I debated on waiting until my hands had more movement in them. Not sure how much alone time I'd been given I gritted my teeth, rocked my body, forcing my knuckles into the ground, giving myself the momentum to flip over. I now faced the fire. Holding my breath, I clenched my teeth against the pain shooting through my limbs and flipped again. I glanced over my shoulder and spied a medium size branch sticking out of the fire, smoldering. I measured the distance between the rope and the branch, then wiggled and pushed my way toward it with the side of my face and shoulder. The movement provided to be excruciatingly difficult.

I stopped. My breath a labored rush. Sweat soaked my face and shirt. The fire ignited a hot blaze on my wrists. I glanced back again, a tremor rocked me. I rested a half inch

195

away from burning a chunk of flesh out of my hand. I needed to push myself up and back. My face stung and my energy was quickly draining. I laid there for a few minutes with tears in my eyes.

Focus Montana, you can do this, my small voice whispered. I blinked the tears away, pulled up as much of my reserves as possible, and shimmied over to the branch.

I touched the rope, holding my arms and legs taut, to the burning branch and felt it give. I jerked my legs down, breaking the rope. I glanced over my shoulder again, making sure I hadn't set myself on fire. The tangled break glared back at me, blackened and scorched.

Massive waves of pain marched up my limbs as the numbness dissipated. *What do I do now?* I knew I should be scared, but my tired brain wouldn't allow the emotion to surface. Fear wasn't an option anyway. I really needed a nap, but I needed to escape too. I almost wished I was scared, the emotion would give me the adrenaline kick I needed. I searched my mind again for the memories that were lost to me. It sure would be nice to know what I was up against, and why I was here.

First things first, I had to get my hands in front of me again. Then I could singe off the ropes around my wrists. I groaned, rolled onto my back, pulled my shoulders back, and brought my arms down. Lifting my hips, I looped my arms around and through my bent knees.

With my arms now in front of me I stretched, examined the rope around my wrists and frowned. The rope was tied so tight around my wrists my hands had a slight purple tint to them. I'd cause myself significant pain burning the rope off. The next best thing to do would be to untie the rope at my ankles, at least then I'd be able to walk.

I bent down to examine the rope better, thinking maybe if I could pull my boots off, the bindings would loosen enough to slide off. I yanked on one of my boots, something shifted against the side of my shin. I pressed my fingers hard against my leg, locating the object. Excited, I tugged at the leg of my jeans until I managed to drag the material through the rope and over my boot.

I blinked my eyes. Blood rushed to my head, my ears buzzed, and my hands started shaking. *A knife*. I freed the blade from my boot and glanced around at my surroundings. The silence would have been eerie if not for the constant crackle and pop of the fire.

I started cutting away at the rope around my ankles. When the rope frayed enough I tugged off my boots, hoping to find more buried treasure. They were empty. I pushed them back on and stretched my weary legs.

Through trial, error, agony from my hands cramping, and only dropping the knife a few times, the rope around my wrists loosened. After getting my hands free I examined my wrists. I'd only sliced my flesh a few times, but not too deep. Actors in movies made cutting through rope look so much easier than it actually was.

I collected the rope, added it to my current stash in my jacket pocket, shook my arms, and moved my fingers and wrists to expel the numbness. The only thing that felt like it received the most damage was my head. Tenderly I touched the back of my skull just above my neck. My fingers ran across a swollen gash with dried blood covering it. I vaguely remembered being knocked unconscious, but

197

couldn't dredge up the full memory. *Was the incident that traumatic or was it where I got hit?* I convinced myself my memories would come back, eventually. Right now I needed to conjure up an escape plan.

As I walked around to the other side of the fire I noticed two tunnels, one to the right, and one ahead of me. Blackness encased the open spaces; I couldn't see anything after a few feet. I leaned against on of the walls, debating on which tunnel to venture into first. I sighed. I needed light before I would step into either of the tunnels. I searched the fire for a good hefty branch as I pulled everything out of my pockets. I thought again about why I was here, before pushing it aside, and reminded myself I needed to stay focused or I might go crazy thinking about my amnesia and the "boogie man" that might be right around the corner.

Flashes of this movie I once watched, about mutant blind albinos. living in cave tunnels, killing everyone, skittered through my mind. My heart began to pound a little harder, great, just what I needed, an overactive imagination. I shook my head, trying to erase the images. I should probably lay off the horror flicks for a while.

My pockets produced the rope, a knife, smokes, lighter, and my cell phone. I stuffed everything but the knife back in the pockets then took off my jacket and one of my shirts. Taking the knife I ripped the bottom of the shirt, cutting it into a rag, yanked my now half shirt back on, along with my jacket, and dug into the fire for the branch I'd seen. I tugged the wood out of the fire, held it up and wrapped the rag around the smoldering tip.

I'd seen this in a couple of movies and hoped it would

work. The shirt smoked for a few seconds before catching on fire. With my knife in one hand and my torch in the other, I stepped into the tunnel in front of me, going with my gut this was the way out. My heart beat in my ears and my stomach dropped in anticipation as I slowly walked through the tunnel, ready for anything that might come at me.

The closer I moved to the end of the tunnel the colder the air became. Chills wracked my body when I finally stumbled to the entrance, or in my case the exit of the cave, a huge bush blocked my way out. I moved a few branches aside, just far enough to notice the inky sky and whiteout conditions. I squinted in an attempt to get a grasp of the location of the cave, but could barely see my hand in front of my face, let alone the rest of the forest. I considered using my cell phone and sighed. I didn't think I'd pick up a signal in this mess and I didn't want to run down the battery trying to get one.

Mumbling more than a few expletives I walked back down the tunnel at a fast pace, until I made it back to the smoke filled fire. I nodded my head in exhaustion. I needed to add more fuel to the dying embers. I didn't want to freeze to death in a cave where no-one would ever find me. I rounded the cave, checking the dark corners, and stumbled upon heavy branches, drug them to the pit, and proceeded to break and stack a few pieces, teepee style, onto the dying blaze. The dry leaves and wood caught quickly and my eyes followed the flames to where I believed would be a ceiling. I'm pretty sure there was a ceiling somewhere up there, but I couldn't see it. Feeling toasty again I took a deep breath before wandering through the opening of the second tunnel.

Halfway down the tunnel, I stepped on something dry and crunchy; I jumped back, picturing cockroaches crawling over the floor. *Did I mention my imagination was working on overtime?* A shiver marched up my spine to the top of my head, making my hair stand on end, bile rose in my throat. I despise cockroaches, they gross me out, and even worse was the sound of them being stepped on. *Yuk.* Another shiver ran up my spine.

I lowered my torch, sweeping it above the floor and close to the walls. Nothing skittered across the rough stone. The floor was different. I swore the floor moved but didn't have enough light to identify what crept under my feet. I took a few soft steps, hearing a crunch with each. Freaked out I ran the short distance to the other smaller cave, praying a huge momma cockroach didn't wait for me inside. Pitch black surrounded me; I crouched down, waving the torch close to the floor.

A crazy women's laughter bubbled from my throat as I sat down to catch my breath. Leaves were scattered throughout the soft dirt. My mind had been playing tricks on me. My nerves took over, shaking uncontrollably a cackle escaped my mouth. Taking big gulps of air I relaxed a little, telling myself I wasn't going to cry. I just needed to wait out the storm, and for daylight for my escape. Once I started breathing normally again I rose and began to search the cave.

My stomach rumbled, my lips were parched. I didn't think I would find any food, but water or a bowl would fill me up for the time being. I followed the same routine I had before, only, this time, I followed the walls. Halfway through the cave, I stumbled upon a big pile of leaves. As I circled around to the front of the pile I realized it was some kind of nest, another small nudge at my memory. I squatted down to look inside, careful not to start the thing on fire.

What I would do for a flashlight right now.

Yuk. Dead bird carcasses.

I moved away from the nest quickly and finished scouting the cave. Besides the burrow of leaves, nothing else stood out.

I returned to the main cave, sat down, and lit a smoke. Something about the nest tickled the back of my brain. I waited for the memory to surface, but it stayed beyond my grasp. Sighing, I forced myself to stand and walk to the cave entrance. I needed water, snow was frozen water. I eyed the trunk of the bush and began to carefully cut a makeshift bowl out of it.

My first attempt rewarded me with a medium size piece of bark. I set the makeshift cup down and sliced out a bigger piece of bark. After scooping fresh snow into both pieces I turned my back on the darkness and blowing snow, trudged to the fire, set the bark down close to the heat, and melted it. I drank the minute amount of water, knew I should collect more, but couldn't convince my body to move another inch. Yawning, I crawled back to the far end of the wall, shoved the knife into my boot, got into the most comfortable position I could, sitting up, and closed my eyes.

My head throbbed, goose bumps needled my flesh. *Why the hell was I so uncomfortable? Oh, yeah, I was stuck in a damn cave.* I swallowed a moan as my sixth

201

sense sounded and alarm, someone had joined me in the cave. My heart skipped a few beats while I debated on whether or not I should continue playing possum. *No, I needed to deal with this head on.* I forced my eyes open, my heart stopped, I blinked, then pinched myself. *What was that thing?*

All of a sudden memories came flooding back at me full force. I crouched in the bushes, gun drawn. Before I got off a shot he pounced, a blur, faster than I'd given him credit for. I vaguely remembered the pain shoot through my skull before he knocked me out. I'd lost my backpack, my gun, and my flashlight too.

I cringed, kept myself from rubbing the bump on my head.

On the positive side Max and Chase would be looking for me, or at least, they will be once the storm blew over. *Was the storm over?* I wish I knew. Now, all I had to do was stay alive until they found me, or I found them.

Until then, I only had a knife to defend myself with. *Could I defend myself with just a knife? Would I have to?*

I grimaced at the thing while studying it. Male, more human than animal, but definitely mutated. A chuckle bubbled up into my throat. I held it in. The last thing I needed was him to attack me because of my nerves.

He reminded me of someone trying to pull off dressing like a big, white, snow clown. Clowns were right up there with cockroaches, except clowns were freaky scary, roaches were freaky gross. I refrained from shaking my head, I'd lost my mind. A snow clown, now that was ridiculous.

A big, mean, snow clown sounded better. About 6'2,

his hair, face, and body were as white as the snow. His clothes, if you could call them that, were skin tight. I took a closer look, scratch clothes, the white, sparkled sheen flowing over his body was an outer layer of skin.

I now understood why I never caught a real glimpse of him. He'd camouflaged himself well, according to nature. I bet if he needed to he would molt, or whatever he did, into the color of the cave.

His eyelashes were crazy long, sparkled white, and covered eyes that bulged out of his head. He had two slits in the sides of his head. *Ears?* I watched him watching me. His eyes moved in an eerie, circular, motion. One eye settled on me, the other scanned the rest of the cave.

His nose was small and angular, with two small slits in them for breathing. I pictured small razor sharp teeth underneath his thin lips. I glanced down at his hands. On both, five fingers fused together into a group of two and a group of three, giving them a tong-like appearance. Nasty claws spiked out of each finger. His bare feet were identical to his hands. I pictured the bruises on my ankles; too similar to be coincidental. He glared unspoken hatred at me.

I wondered again if my knife would be enough to take him out.

I'd never seen anything quite like him and hoped I never would again. I didn't pick up any violence in him at this moment, just hate and curiosity. Not one muscle moved in my body. I waited patiently to see if he intended to make the first move. When nothing happened I sat up straighter, attempting to get semi comfortable. My back was killing me, and my bones ached from leaning up against the wall.

In slow motion, I unbent one leg and stretched it out before bending it back up. I didn't want my knife to be too far out of reach. I did the same with my other leg, both of my arms, my neck, and my back, keeping my eye on the psycho-mutant-creature the whole time. He'd taken an alert stance while I stretched. We remained staring at each other for so long I thought I would die of stiffness and boredom. Suddenly he turned on his heel and walked through door number one, towards the exit.

My heart caught in my throat. *Was he leaving again? Please let him leave!* I exhaled long, slow, breaths, waiting for what seemed like an eternity before I got up. I did a full stretch on my aching muscles and stuck my knife up my sleeve. For whatever reason he wanted me here he certainly didn't seem interested in feeding me, or hurting me, at this point anyway. I picked up my bark and slowly tiptoed through the tunnel. I didn't need my torch to see light outside. Maybe my new friend dropped off the face of the earth, and I would be able to escape.

As I walked through the tunnel my momentum began to slow down. *How long had I been gone?* I didn't know if I was two or three days into this fiasco because I had no idea how long I'd been unconscious. My stomach behaved as though it had been a week. I shuddered at the thought. That would mean that Max and Chase weren't coming or something bad may have happened to them. *What if I gave them too many sleeping pills?* I shook my head, I'd only added a couple to their drinks.

Bringing myself back from the worst case scenario I concentrated on the positive. I had water. I reached the bush, happy I hadn't been jumped, and peeked out. Still snowing. I collected as much snow as possible, plus a couple of leaves, and headed back to the fire thinking about Max. As many times as I wished he'd vanish, I really needed his help now.

Ignoring the hunger pains, I melted the snow, drank it, then made several more trips back to the bush. I brushed my mega fuzzy teeth the best I could with the leaves while dreaming of a nice hot bath in my Jacuzzi. By the time I made my last trip to the entrance the snow had subsided into flurries, but the sun sat low on the horizon. I sighed; another night stuck in the cave.

I whipped my cell phone out of my pocket and pushed the power button. Nothing happened. I pushed on the power button again for a couple of seconds longer. Still nothing. I checked to make sure the battery was still in my phone, it was. *Damn!* I must have forgotten to charge it. I glared at the overcast clouds. *No, I specifically remembered plugging it in.* Hell, the charger probably wasn't plugged into the wall. Or the phone may have been on, while I lay unconscious, searching for a signal. That would drain the battery quickly. I heaved a long sigh. Whatever happened I was minus a phone. My mind blurred from hunger, my head throbbed, I was sore, exhausted, and my escape plan had been thwarted today.

Frustrated, I plopped the stupid thing back into my pocket, instead of throwing it at the wall. I separated the branches of the bush. Nothing looked familiar, but if my vision still worked correctly, and I hoped I wasn't hallucinating, smoke puffed up from a chimney in the distance. I smiled. A house. Darkness settled into the sky, leaving now wasn't an option, but that was the direction I'd be heading in, come dawn. I returned to my spot in the cave, sat with my back against the wall, and lit a smoke.

I didn't understand why he wanted me, but I could come up with several reasons. The one thing I was certain, my life was in danger. Anger coursed through my veins. And since anger was a lot better than despair I grabbed hold of the emotion, lit another smoke, and stewed until finally I was emotionally drained enough to sleep.

Chapter Twenty-One

I woke up abruptly. The dream about Max coming to my rescue, fading. I laughed. I didn't plan on waiting for him. I surveyed the inside of the cave and shivered. I'd forgotten to put wood on the fire.

Not sensing my friend I stood up and added a couple of logs to the sputtering embers. I needed to get out of here quick, but wasn't going to get far if I didn't stretch out my aching limbs first. My movement was stiffer than I wanted it to be. Besides it was cold outside, I wanted a little warmth before I left. I did a few yoga stretches to limber up, warmed my hands, and then looked around again to make sure I was alone.

I blew out a breath, it was now or never. I pulled my knife out of my boot and slid it up my sleeve. I had a plan, as soon as I stepped out of the cave entrance I'd run like the devil was chasing me. I took in the darkness of the tunnel, still night, didn't matter, I was out of here.

I relied on my senses as I placed my hand on the cave wall, and took small steps towards the exit. The nearer I got to my escape route the lighter it became. I'd be able to see the terrain once I left the cover of the bush. A sigh of relief passed through my lips. I made it to the bush unscathed, glimpsed out. Smoke still rose in the distance. I didn't sense my friend. Taking a deep breath to steady my nerves I focused on the direction of the rising smoke, stepped out from behind the bush, and took off down the steep incline, leading away from the cave.

I ran as fast as my still stiff body would allow, tripping over rocks and logs buried under the snow every few feet. My pace slowed a touch, to avoid breaking my neck. I was heading down the hill at a good pace when my foot slid and flew out from under me. My arms flapped in the wind, trying to catch my balance. I failed miserably, landed hard on my hip, and slid the rest of the way downhill. There was nothing to grab hold of and I must have hit every single sharp rock on the way down. I felt so badly bruised by the time I came to a stop that I had a hard time standing back up.

Wiping snow from my clothes, I ran, gimped, and walked in the direction I thought I should go in. The plume of smoke was no longer visible through the forest of trees, so I had to rely on my "ha-ha" excellent sense of direction. I'd made it a good distance from the cave and almost to the tree line when my alarm rang. He closed in on me.

Shit! I couldn't let him corner me again.

Before my thoughts could process an escape route he flew up behind me, grabbed my hair, and yanked it hard enough to bring me to a full stop. My legs flew out from underneath me; I was flat on my ass again with my loving, psycho, snow clown, pulling me back up the steep slope I'd just come down. I let my body go limp as he dragged me by my hair and jacket through the bush, into the cave, and to

208

the fire.

The bump on the back of my head shot pain through my skull. A trickle of sticky, wet, blood, oozed down the back of my neck.

He dumped me in the same spot I'd first found myself, facing the wall. His eyes burned a hole in my back, with a mixture of anger and amusement. I grasped a hold of his anger, making it my own, as I laid there waiting to see what he would do next. Once again we were having a staring contest. The only difference, this time, he was the only one staring. I played possum, again.

I hoped he stared at me for the next hour. It would give me time for the pain in my head to abate, and the nausea in my stomach to go away. The longer he gazed at me the more his anger grew. My head calmed to a hateful throb, my stomach had settled on just being queasy when I sensed and barely heard him turn on his heel. I slid the knife out my sleeve into my hand, flipped over onto my feet, and lunged onto his back, holding on tight.

Pain laced through my chest and stomach from the small razor sharp horns on his back. I hadn't noticed them before. I began to bleed almost immediately. The sharp edges stung like hell, but I held on tight as he tried to throw me off. He swung around, backing up towards the cave wall as I swung the blade under, and up, attempting to get a stab in his chest. He blocked me, grabbed hold of my wrist, and shook it hard a couple of times. I held fast to the knife. While his attention was diverted I dug my knees into his sides hard, wrapped my arm around his neck, getting a choke hold, and squeezed. He dropped my wrist and dug his claws through my jacket, into my arm, pulling it away

209

from his neck.

Shocked, and in pain I jumped off him, cringing at the sucking noise my skin made as it ripped free of his horns. Amazingly I landed on my feet. I backed up, looking at the gashes on my arm quickly, blood seeped out, the marks inflamed and burning. I glanced back up at my captor and swore he was smiling.

His lips were pulled back over his teeth, reminding me of a barracuda, jagged and sharp. A burning sensation began to climb up my arm, making me wonder if he had some kind of poison in his claws. That pissed me off. If I was going down so was he. I ran at him, catching him off guard, and kicked him hard in the stomach. He landed flat on his ass, I smiled at him in triumph. It was about time someone else ended up down there besides me.

He jumped back up and shouldered me in the ribs, knocking the wind out of me. I landed on my hands and knees close to the fire. Breathing hard I grabbed a burning log and swung it full throttle against his leg. The smell of burnt flesh filled my nose. He jumped back and came at me again, slashing his claws across my side as I brought the blade up and sliced diagonally from his kidney to his navel, drawing blood. My side was on fire now, and dizziness started to flow through me, giving me a sense of vertigo. I blinked my eyes a few times to bring them back into focus, rolled onto my feet, jumped up, and kneed him with all my strength in the area where I was hoping his nads would be. He dropped to the ground wheezing. I stood there for a moment trying to catch my breath.

As I took a step forward, my eyes blurred and my head began to swim. I stepped back, leaned against the wall, blinking my eyes fiercely until I got my vision back, and seemed steadier. That minute gave him all the time he needed to recover and come at me again. In one swift motion, I slid down the wall and brought the knife up, stabbing him in the stomach, and twisting it as far into his gut as the blade would allow. He fell heavily on top of me.

The burning from the gashes on my arm progressed to my shoulder, and the burning from my side slowly forged its way down my leg, making it difficult for me to move. The torn flesh on my chest stung.

I sat there with tears in my eyes. I needed to move, to get home and clean out my wounds before they became worse. With the remaining strength I had, I pushed him off of me and onto the floor. My hands shook as I pulled the rope out of my pocket.

My vision blurred, again. I shook my head hard to clear it, making myself nauseous in the process. The ground under me shifted and trails of light flickered around me. His chest rose with shallow breaths. As quick as I could I tied the pieces of rope together though I felt like I was moving in slow motion. Carefully I flipped him onto his stomach with my foot, avoiding blatantly staring at the big pool of blood gurgling out of him, and pulled his hands behind his back. Just the sight of the spikes, not horns, on his back covered with my blood made me sick. I swallowed hard and tightly bound his wrists together. I took the scarf off my neck, wondering how I managed not to get strangled with it, and tied it tight around his ankles, bringing it up and tying it to the rope around his wrists in the same fashion he'd tied me. After that was done I crawled over to the fire and attempted to empty my stomach. With no food

211

and little water, I only managed dry heaves.

Dizziness consumed me. I wasn't going to make it out. I was burning up. I crawled to the back side of the fire, away from the mutant thing and laid down. The pain and burning from his claws was getting worse. I took note of the damage. My whole arm and side were red and inflamed and it was spreading. I sighed. I glance at the exit, only being able to see a few feet ahead of me.

My last thought was I'd figure out what to do right after I rested. I rolled over to my semi unhurt side with my back to the fire and closed my eyes.

Chapter Twenty-Two

"She's over here Max! And she's burning up!"

Was that Chase's voice?

Several hands caressed my body.

"We need to get her home. Call the doc and have him meet us there." A hoarse voice replied.

Was that Max? Did he sound scared? I tried to open my eyes, they were too heavy. *Was I dreaming of getting rescued?* If so I didn't want it to end, just a few more minutes and I'd wake up.

"It's over. You're going to be fine, Montana," Chase whispered in my ear. "Man look at all this blood."

"Over here!" Max yelled. "It looks like she did a number on him. We need to take him too. Go get the extra gear while I get some pictures."

"The Doc should be here soon. I'm really worried, Max, she's got some major gouges in her flesh."

"I'll get her upstairs, send Doc up when he gets here, and keep an eye on her captor."

Their voices drifted over the low hum in my head. I tried to sit up, open my eyes, speak. Nothing on my body

213

would budge. Even thinking took much effort at this point.

Max lifted me gently and carried me to the bed. He removed my clothes, and wiped my skin off with a warm, wet, cloth, starting with my feet, and covering me with a blanket as he worked his way up. The cloth became cooler the closer he got to my face. The gentle caress relaxed my aching muscles; I started dreaming about that bath again.

Ouch, that hurt. Another stabbing pain, another pinprick. I jerked my leg up, hitting something.

Light laughter.

"Hold her down so you do not get kicked again."

"Is she going to be all right?"

"I honestly cannot tell you right now Max. She has lost a lot of blood, has a high fever, and has too much poison pumping through her system. Not to mention she is dehydrated and has not had any food. How long did you say she was missing?" The doctor replied.

"Five days. Between the last storm and pinpointing the location from the GPS signal on her phone it took us that long to find her."

"If she makes it through this it is going to take time for her health to come back. Hold her arm down so I do not get punched, I am going to get an IV in her with some fluids and antibiotics. The painkillers will have to wait until we figure out what kind of poison has caused this."

He inserted a needle into my arm, making me cringe inwardly.

"After I get this set up we will go downstairs and extract some of the poison out of.., well out of that thing down there."

"Get as many samples as you need before the morning.

That's when I'll be taking him back."

What! That thing was in my house! I want it out of my house! I wanted to scream at Max to kill it and take it to the dump. I want to scream at him not to leave.

He planted a light kiss on my lips before they left the room. I fell back into a fitful sleep, waking up periodically to rustling noises around me.

The next time I came around pressure was being applied to my wounds. I waited for the pain to follow, but nothing happened. I opened my eyes. Even though my vision was still blurry the first person to come into view was Max. He sat next to me on the bed, holding my hand. His handsome, rugged face was a sight for sore eyes. I wanted to rub my fingers through the thick whiskers covering his chin, but my hand wouldn't lift off the bed, and the many emotions flowing through him made my head swim.

I sighed and redirected my attention to the doctor. He bent over me, the epitome of calm, applying pressure to my scrapes and gouges. I tried to turn my head in his direction and found my head refused to move. I wanted to ask why, but I was too doped up to get the words from my mind to my lips, so I looked at him questionably.

"I have got it immobilized for the time being. You were thrashing around and I didn't want it re-injured."

Could he read minds? I glanced at Max. He looked really haggard, but nodded at me and smiled.

"Max wants to know what happened. I told him not to get his hopes up about you talking right now. I am glad to see that you are awake." The Doc smiled. "I think I have been able to get your fever under control, for now anyway.

215

You are beat up pretty bad and have a slight concussion."
He rolled his chair closer to me, and stared into my eyes,
making sure I understood what he was saying. "Those are
the least of your concerns."

Boy, the Doc looked old and wiped out this close-up. I
focused on his lips in an attempt to comprehend his words;
my brain was already floating away.

"Every time he scratched you he injected poison into
you from his claws."

That made sense.

"I believe I have figured out what kind of poison and I
am working on treating it, but he managed to pump a good
amount into your body…."

I felt like I was disembodied, I couldn't concentrate on
his words anymore, so I closed my eyes. The last thing I
heard was the doctor telling Max that it would be touch and
go for a while. I swam to the surface again in time to hear
Max talking.

"I have to go. I'll keep in touch. I've asked the Doc to
do a few more blood tests after the poisons out of her
system to see if there's some kind of cure for whatever my
employers pumped into her. Keep me informed."

A light kiss wafted over my cheek.

"Will do, I'll keep an eye on everything for you. Take
care Max."

Chase sat down and grasped my hand. "You're going
to be as good as new soon, I promise."

I drifted off again.

This was new. I stood beside my bed watching myself
thrash as sweat poured down my body. Chase slept in a

chair next to me, worn out. I glanced over at myself. It didn't look like I was doing so well. I hated to wake Chase, but I needed the Doc. I reached over to nudge Chase. My fingers sunk into the flesh of his shoulder. *Wow. That was kind of cool.* I tried again. My hand emerged through the back of his shoulder, tingling unnaturally, unreal, and funky. I pulled it out of his shoulder quickly.

I sighed. I needed to get his attention, but how? I thought about it as my breathing got shallower by the minute. If something happened to me he would never forgive himself. I stepped in front of him and screamed as loud as I could. We had a connection; I hoped he would hear me somehow. It worked better than I thought it would. He jumped up and right through me a split second before screaming for the Doc. I shuddered at the weird sensation of our energies mixing for that brief second.

I heard the Doc run up the stairs at an extremely fast pace for an old guy. He came barreling into the room. If I had to guess his age, I'd say about 110, which was ancient to me. He was of Indian descent, with long gray hair, add a few black strands to that, parted perfectly, and braided down his back. He also had the sharpest, most amazing, light blue eyes I've ever seen.

I swore his gazed landed on me right before he stepped in front of my body and shouted out demands to Chase. I tried to peek over his shoulder to see what he was doing but he blocked my every move. I also tried to walk over to the other side of the bed, but apparently I was attached to my body because I could only wander a few feet before I got yanked back to my original spot.

I focused on Doc and Chase and found their

217

movements chaotic. Chase skidded into the bathroom for a cool, wet, cloth, and started patting my skin down. Doc checked my vital signs with quick deliberate motions. Chase raced out of the bedroom, only to come back with something that smelled and looked horrific. Green and brown goo, reminding me of something that came out of a sick baby's bottom, filled a pestle and mortar set. The Doc began slathering my body with it.

Yuk!

I'd be better off back in my body, not knowing what he was doing.

I attempted to dive back into my body. I rejected myself. *How weird was that?* My body didn't want me, yet if I walked too far away from it I got yanked back. Now, that was too much to wrap my mind around. I focused on the Doc again. He was checking my IV and the other miscellaneous needles and tubes he'd hooked me up to. He nodded, content he'd done everything he could, sent Chase out of the room, sat down, and stared at me. Not my body, but me.

I stood my ground as we kept an eye on each other for the next few hours. The only interruption: his getting up periodically to make sure my body still breathed. Chase came in and out of the room several times, and I listened to him leave a message on Max's cell phone, giving him an update on my condition.

It's amazing how easy it is to stay standing for so long when you don't have a body that gets tired, too bad I couldn't go very far.

The next time the Doc got up to check on me I snagged his seat and kicked my legs up onto my bed. He gazed over at me and sat on his rolling chair. *Huh, he really did see me.*

"So does everyone call you Doc or do you have a real name?" I asked sarcastically. I wasn't trying to be rude. I was just a tad bit annoyed with my predicament.

"I will tell you when you return to your body," he replied.

Wow, he heard me.

"I don't feel like it, it hurts too much in there, especially when the pain killers wear off."

"So that is why you are out here? The pain killers wore off?"

I shrugged; I had no idea why my body rejected me. "Could be, it doesn't matter. I'm not planning on going anywhere." I glanced at the empty shell that used to hold my spirit. "Maybe I just needed a physical and mental break. Tell me about Max." I said, changing the subject.

"He will tell you himself when he gets back."

I laughed. Max was as secretive as they came.

"Hey, Doc, who are you talking to?" Chase asked, coming into the room.

Doc glanced at Chase, "Montana. Come, sit in my chair and keep her company."

Doc avoided my gaze.

"Keep her comfortable, she is starting to get cranky. I need to go down and make some more paste."

"Ooh, my very own voodoo doctor." I really couldn't help myself.

Chase waited until the Doc left the room before whispering in my ear. "I should have known you were going to go out and play hero. I'd hoped you and Max

219

would come to a compromise, but apparently that wasn't the case."

I stood at my side of the bed and leaned over towards him. If the Doc could hear me maybe Chase could too. "I'm so sorry, Chase. He didn't want me involved."

Chase didn't acknowledge me.

He blew out a breath and grabbed my hand. "I could have stopped this if I'd said something to Max, but I didn't." He lowered his head for a moment, moving closer to me. "He really is a good guy. A little over protective of you. Okay, a lot overprotective, but he's still a good guy. The only reason I didn't tell him was because he most likely would of duck taped you to a chair, which wouldn't have helped matters."

He grinned wide for a few seconds and chuckled. I was sure he was imagining me bound to a chair. They would have had to gag me too.

"What were you thinking Montana?" Chase asked, serious again.

"I was thinking I would handle it, and I did. Max has him now; he can't threaten me anymore or anyone else." I knew Chase didn't hear me but continued anyway. "He could have taken you out in the blink of an eye, Chase, and what about Rose, or the girls? He was a threat and needed to be dealt with."

A low vibrating sounded from his pocket. Chase let go of my hand to answer his cell. "Max?"

Silence on our end. What I would have given to be able to listen in on the conversation.

"She's had a setback. No, the Doc didn't tell me, but her fever has come back," Silence. "He's downstairs cooking up his concoctions." More silence. "Okay, I'll call tomorrow unless something else happens. Okay. Okay." He flipped his phone shut.

"Max is worried about you. He'll be back once he gets this worked out." Chase sighed. "I'm worried about you too."

"Don't worry about me Chase. I'll be fine." I wasn't worried about me.

"Hey Doc, would you please tell him that I'm going to be fine," I said as the Doc wandered back into the room.

He just glanced at me and asked Chase to move.

"Seriously, just tell him!"

Doc asked Chase to get something downstairs and then glared at me.

"There is a problem with that."

"What's the problem?"

"You are not in any pain out here. Who is to say that you will not stay?"

Chase came back up with whatever it was the Doc needed.

"It's not like I can just jump back into my body. I'm not going to die or go into a coma or anything. Trust me on this one."

He leaned over my body and raised an eyebrow at me Chase wouldn't see.

"Chase would understand."

He shook his head subtly and began to redress my wounds. There was nothing left to do but wait, and since Chase had taken my chair I was back to standing up. I stuck my tongue out at Doc and paced the few steps I could.

"I'm bored. We need a TV. Chase should take my

221

truck to Max's or something so no one knows I'm here. Or maybe he should tell anyone who stops by he had to drop me off at the airport. I had to leave for an emergency or something." I stopped pacing. "You should tell Chase I'm standing here in spirit and relay my messages."

A sigh from the Doc.

"I'm not trying to drive you crazy." I smiled big. "Chase would talk to me if he knew. I need some comedy."

"We need a TV up here," Chase stated. "Maybe some zombie movies will bring her back. She loves those."

"See its ESP or something," I said, laughing and clapping my hands together.

The Doc turned to Chase. "I need some things anyway. I will write you a list. I suggest some comedy instead of horror. I am sure she has seen enough of that lately."

I sat down in the chair Chase evacuated and evaluated my empty shell. I looked like hell. I leaned in closer, examining my wounds.

The red streaks spreading out from the gashes seemed to be disappearing, and the swelling was going down, most likely from the goop covering them. My bruises were fading, leaving black, blue, and ugly yellow smudges against my skin. My temperature had gone down too, sweat glistened on my skin, instead of pouring out of my pores. I attempted to rest my hand on my forehead to see if I was still running a fever. My hand flew back.

I wasn't welcome back into my shell, yet. Yet, being the operative word. At least, I was starting to heal. With nothing better to do than wait, I closed my eyes and rejoiced in the pain-free, stress-free environment I'd found myself stuck in.

Chapter Twenty-Three

"You need to open your eyes and stay alert."

"Why?" I asked, keeping my eyes shut. Sleep didn't seem to be an option in spirit form.

"Because I do not want you disappearing into the nether land."

"That's not going to happen." I glanced at him. "I'm healing."

"Yes, but your spirit is still out here."

"Only for another day or two." I wasn't about to tell him my body didn't want me back. The Doc gave me a questioning glance, leaned over my wounds, and started wiping off and reapplying the goop. "How am I doing?"

"Fever is going down, bruises and head are healing. My special paste is sucking the poison out of your system; unfortunately, the process is slower than I had hoped for, and you are still dehydrated. Might be because of the poison, but I am not sure. Now, the shot they gave you? I have no idea. It is not showing up in your blood work and Max is not going to be happy about that."

"That may be the reason I'm not in my body right now. With everything else going on, feeling unnecessary

223

emotion might be too much to handle."

"Hey, Doc, who are you talking to?" Chase asked from the doorway.

Doc glared at me. "Just talking out loud."

"I picked up the TV and the stuff on your list. Do you have a few minutes to help me out with it?"

"Sure."

They disappeared down the stairs, brought up the flat screen a few minutes later, and hung the TV in the corner of my room, beside my dresser, on a mount. It was pretty cool. The mount swiveled in and out, so I could adjust it as needed. Now I had the opportunity to lie in bed all day, zoning out on meaningless shows. I've rarely found anything worthwhile on TV to watch.

Chase slid a comedy into the DVD player he'd also bought and hit play.

The Doc vacated his seat to go do whatever he does in my kitchen. Chase plopped down in it, getting comfortable. The comedy blared on the screen. Chase adjusted the volume, and soon we were laughing so hard our breathing became erratic.

This went on for days. I'd pay close attention to the process of getting better, then regressing again. Chase and I would watch a comedy. I'd pace, and when no-one was looking I'd try and dive back into my body.

A week passed. Two weeks passed. It all seemed so surreal. The Doc kept a good eye on both of us, taking great care of my beat up body while making sure I didn't float away into never-never land. I'd always considered myself tough, but as the days flew by I started to get nervous.

Was I ever going to get better?

224

Max called every day to make sure I was still alive. How sweet of him, I thought, grudgingly. I wondered what he could possibly be doing that was taking him so long to get back. Then reminded myself that I really didn't care. He was no longer here, which meant he could no longer cause me any trouble.

Max had known the psycho, snow clown was an experiment gone wrong, but recently found out he was one of Max's old friends. The agency informed Max, over a year ago, Blake died on a mission.

His experimental friend had been resuscitated and mutated into what the government hoped would be the perfect assassin. Able to blend in with his surroundings, get behind enemy lines, and kill everyone in his way. Until he escaped, that is.

They'd sent Max to find, Blake, the assassin, hoping it would be an easy job, considering they'd been friends. What they didn't take into consideration was that Blake would recognize Max. All of Blake's past memories were, to their knowledge, wiped clean. But Blake's memories started coming back to him the more he saw Max. Because of the way he was now engineered Max became the enemy. When I walked into the picture, some fuse popped, making the situation worse.

I had no doubt Max would have found him and recaptured him had he not felt the need to protect me. But with me in the picture the situation wasn't as optimal for Max as it had been. Eventually, Blake would have killed me and Max, or whoever he got his claws in first. Afterwards he might have gone after Chase and Rose,

225

spreading out to the people who lived up here in the mountains.

The government may have been able to engineer a great assassin, but they definitely couldn't control it. The answer to whether Blake was dead or alive stayed classified, along with the knowledge of whether they were experimenting on him again. I didn't think Max was even privy to the information.

Max also said he wasn't coming back until he found a cure for the shot they gave me, which his government buddies denied having anything to do with.

Chase whispered the details to me one night, hoping an explanation might help me to get it together. I hoped so too, but apparently not. I still paced around in spirit form. It was nice not having to worry about eating or sleeping, but at the same time, I was ready to get on with my life.

Chase changed into his Santa outfit and dressed Killer in his elf outfit. Killer thumped his tail on my bed, ready to go. I grinned, Killer, would have a blast around the kids. Chase moaned about leaving my side. The Doc ended up kicking him out the door, with the presents we'd bought for the kids. He explained, again, to Chase, it would be good for him to be away from me for a while. I, on the other hand, was ecstatic to get out of attending the Christmas party, even if it meant I was stuck in bed.

The Doc glared at me, shaking his head. He was ready for me to nose dive back into my body. Honestly, so was I. I'd finally broken the fever and was healing nicely. The poison was almost completely out of my system and I was on the road to recovery. Doc had added something, to fade the big, ugly scars from the gashes to my daily regimen. The good news: the balm had worked on the spike marks on my chest and stomach. Those had disappeared completely.

Chase stumbled in late that night, more than a little drunk. He landed hard on my bed, flopped his arm over me, and passed out with his butt up in the air and his knees slightly tucked under him. His feet dangled over the side of the bed. I tried to push his butt down to make him more comfortable but just like before my hands sunk into his muscles.

The next morning when my phone rang, Chase jumped and crashed to the floor. I laughed. The Santa beard had twisted to the side of his face during the night. The hat hung halfway off his head. His left boot was skewed around facing the wrong direction, and now he laid on his back, arms tucked under him, on the floor, looking like he'd been hit by a mack truck.

He snaked one of his arms out from underneath his back and fumbled with the phone for a minute. The bland expression on his face was priceless. He moaned, scrubbed his other hand over his face and through his hair, attempting to get his brain to work again.

"Chase, are you all right? Is everything all right there? Where's Montana?"

"Yeah, yeah, everything's good here. Montana's down with the flu and you just woke me up."

Rose giggled, "I heard you had a little too much fun at the party last night, that's why I waited until 11 to call."

Chase frowned, glanced at the clock, then glanced at the phone. I was wondering when he was going to figure it

227

out.

"Hold on Rose," he said as he turned the speaker off.

"Are you still there?" Chase asked.

"No, you don't need to come home early, she's fine."

"She's sleeping right now."

"Yes, I'll have her call you as soon as she can. Merry Christmas to you too."

"All right, bye."

Chase hung up the phone and crawled into the bathroom. I listened to him get sick, flush the toilet, and turn on the shower. When he stepped out of the bathroom the Doc handed him something that smelled noxious.

"Drink it."

Chase cringed at the thought.

"Drink it," the Doc growled.

Plugging his nose, Chase drank the murky liquid in three gulps, before running back into the bathroom. The Doc chuckled, aiming his twinkling eyes at me.

"He will not get sick again. He will feel better within ten minutes." Chuckling again he headed back downstairs.

Chase walked out of the bathroom a little green, holding his stomach.

"I'm not drinking again anytime soon," he said to no one in particular.

After about ten minutes he got up from my bed and stretched the kinks out of his muscles.

"I need the recipe for that potion," Chase mumbled as his phone rang.

"Hey girl, how's it going?"

Alexis giggled through the phone.

"Merry Christmas to you too."

Since I couldn't go anywhere I was privy to Chase's side of the conversation, it made me blush.

After the graphic sex talk, Chase grinned wide, blushed. "Montana? Yeah, she's here, but she's sick. I'll have her call you. Don't be a stranger." He hung up and chuckled.

My phone rang.

"Hello."

"Hi, you must be Rita. I'm Chase, a friend of Montana's."

"Yes, just a friend."

"I'm not sure she's ready to settle down yet."

"No, I don't think she's dating anyone."

That was just like my mom, to grill someone else about my love life.

"The casino with the girls, huh."

"No, she's not available right now," He repeated the same story, promising I'd call when I was better.

As the day wore on I started to worry about my sister. She hadn't called yet, and it wasn't like I could pick up the phone and call her. This whole situation was upsetting. I wanted to answer my own phone; to talk to my family. I wanted to go outside and feel the sun on my face. I lunged at my body and bounced right back to where I'd been standing. *Damn it.* I was cursing myself when my phone finally rang.

"Hello," Chase answered.

"Who is this?" My sisters voice boomed on the other end.

Chase went through the same spiel again. Zoë grilled him about our relationship. Chase smirked; getting a real

229

kick out of the conversation until something made him frown.

"What happened to Charlie?"

"A new bike for Christmas."

"The emergency room."

I wanted to smack Chase and have him put the phone on speaker, so I could listen in. I moved closer to him.

"I'm sorry to hear that. Is she all right?"

"Good."

"Actually, she's not available. She's sleeping off the flu."

"I promise she'll call as soon as she can."

He hung up and tapped me on the head with his knuckles.

"You have to wake up now, Montana, Charlie needs to talk to you." He sighed. "Your sister's husband thought it would be great to give her a new bike for Christmas. Of course, Charlie was thrilled and insisted they take her to the park where she promptly broke her arm. She'd convinced them she was adult enough and didn't need the training wheels." He smiled. "Sounds like your niece has a little daredevil in her. Anyway, you need to call her back so she can brag about it to you."

He thumped my head again, then got up to turn on the TV. "I hope I'm done talking to your family for the day."

He sat in my chair, leaving me standing, and closed his eyes. His phone rang. He ignored it. After a few minutes, it rang again. Letting out a long exhale he checked the caller ID.

"Hi, Max."

"Same to you."

"No, she's still the same."

"No, the Doc promises she'll be fine. I'm sure he knows something we don't."

"No, he says she's all there and not to worry about any brain damage or anything."

That was a relief to hear.

"Yeah, the poisons close to fully out of her system."

"No, he can't get rid of the scarring."

"Okay, I'll talk to you tomorrow."

Chase leaned over and smacked me on the head this time. "I'm tired of reporting the same thing every day. I feel like a broken record so get your shit together."

Okay. I got the hint, vacation time was over. Chase closed his eyes and soon fell into a deep sleep. I sat by my body, wondering how I was going to get back in.

Chapter Twenty-Four

I woke up the next morning to a firm slap on the cheek.

"Ouch, what was that for? And what the hell did you blow on me last night?"

"It is about damn time."

"Did you really have to slap me?"

"I did not see you this morning and I could not get you to wake up."

I gazed around the room. My fingertips traced a line up my scars.

"I'm back! It was that powder you blew in my face wasn't it."

"You are, and the first thing you're going to do is get into the shower. You stink."

If he didn't want to admit to bringing me back, it was fine by me. It wasn't important. I knew he had.

I grinned, "Thanks a lot, Doc."

He nodded, wrapped my robe around me the best he could, and headed downstairs to get Chase.

"You're up!" Chase almost screamed.

His high energy and emotions made me cringe. No wonder I'd left my body for so long. I'd forgotten what it felt like.

Chase started to lean down to give me a hug when the Doc put his hand on Chase's shoulder.

"Tone it down about twenty notches," he said, pointing at me.

"Oh shit, I forgot. I'm sorry." His emotions went from excitement to anxiety as he bolted out of the room.

"Give him a moment to collect himself," Doc said.

"So how do you do it?" His energy was calm.

"I will teach you along with your physical therapy. I have not found anything in your blood work, so I cannot give you a cure-all shot. It will take patience and practice."

He said it like I was the most impatient person on earth. Well, maybe I was, but I'd find the patience to have the calm that he carried.

Chase walked back up the stairs more grounded than the first time, strode over to me, and squeezed me so hard I thought I might pass out.

"Get on the other side of her. We are going to help her up."

I finally got my bath. I leaned against the tub while the Doc filled it with water. He helped me into the tub, turned on the jets, then gave me Alexis' product to add. I slid into the water, covering my head, and stayed there for a moment, letting the hot liquid sooth my stiff muscles. I vowed to never take my Jacuzzi for granted again.

I reveled in the tub until I was a prune, dressed in sweat pants and a shirt, and let Doc help me back into bed. The sheets were clean, the pillows fluffed, and I almost felt human again.

"That is enough exercise for right now. We will work on your muscles again in a few hours."

The Doc left as Chase walked in, carrying a tray. He grinned wide and placed it on my lap. I scanned over the food, lightly buttered toast, water, and espresso. My mouth watered. My stomach growled.

"The Doc says to take it slow. He's not sure how you're going to do with real food yet."

"Okay," I tried not to cram the whole piece of toast into my mouth, but it tasted wonderful. I sipped on the coffee between bites and finished the water.

"Where's breakfast? I think you brought me up an empty plate," I grinned.

"You don't get anything else right now. Let's see how that sits."

My stomach growled, louder this time. "Do you hear that? I'm starving."

Chase laughed and handed me my smokes.

"Thanks." I lit one. "Have you talked to Max yet?"

"No. He'll call me later." Chase shrugged his shoulders. Then went into detail about how they'd woken up late the next afternoon, way to groggy to realize what had happened.

I cringed, "I'm sorry, Chase."

Chase gave me a half-hearted glare. "By the time we shook off the drugs it was late. Max searched the house. When he couldn't locate you he went outside to search. He found your backpack and gun buried in the snow. I think he was about ready to panic. By that time, it was dark and starting to snow again. We couldn't do anything. He paced all night, periodically checking the GPS for a signal on

234

your phone. We hoped the storm blocked the signal and nothing else. The next morning blizzard conditions covered the mountains, but we headed back out to the spot where he'd found your backpack anyway. He dug up the fresh snow, hoping there would be something there to lead us to you, and found blood." Chase glared at me.

"Max just about hit the roof, Montana. I've never seen him so pissed and scared at the same time. All we could do was go back to the house and wait for it to stop snowing." He took a deep breath. "I don't think I've ever seen it snow this much in one winter. After the storm blew over we were able to pinpoint where you were located, but we still had to plow ourselves out of the house. We ended up hiking over to Max's house, through knee deep snow, to pick up the snowmobiles. Unfortunately, once we arrived at his house we needed to change, warm up, and eat. Then the snowmobiles wouldn't start. When we finally got them up and running the sun was setting. We ended up driving the snowmobiles back to your place and waited until sunrise to leave. What happened up there? When we arrived there was blood everywhere. It looked like you almost escaped. We followed the trail you both left in the snow on our way up to the cave."

He gave me a questioning glance as he waited for an answer.

"I got tired of being starved to death, so I fought back."

"Well, you did a damn good job." He sighed. "It's too bad you were badly injured in the process."

I smirked. "I still bagged the bad guy."

"A big part of me wants to yell at you for pulling that stunt, but after talking to Max I'm kind of glad you did."

235

He held up his thumb and finger, separating them a little, to show me the amount he was glad. It wasn't much.

"Anyhow we brought you home, and you've been out of it since." Chase went on to describe everything that happened since I'd been on "vacation," which I pretty much already knew. I decided not to tell him about my out of my body experience but was tempted when he omitted Blake staying at the house.

After he finished the story I opted for a short catnap, before the Doc came back to begin my physical therapy.

Physical therapy provided to be excruciatingly painful, instead of giving me a break after; Doc went straight into meditation mode.

"Once you are very good at meditating I will show you how to use it all of the time. It will help you keep other people's emotions away from you."

I feigned napping when Chase entered my room with Max on the phone. I knew I owed Max an explanation for finding me, and a thank you for bringing me home and hiring the Doc to take care of me, but I was still pissed at him and his government world. After Chase left I called my family and assured them I was fine.

It only took a few days before I was up walking on my own, and a few more before I could manage the stairs more than once a day. I was determined to get healthy again.

I began practicing Yoga after a week of physical therapy and began to utilize it with the meditation. Every once in a while, I'd open myself up to get a glimpse of other people's emotions, but like the Doc kept saying "other people's feelings should be their own."

I had to talk to Max or be nagged by Chase until the

236

day I died. Max didn't ask me about what happened, which seemed strange, but he did ask me several times if I was all right and mentioned he was still searching for a cure.

"The Doc has been teaching me self-preservation skills, thanks for sending him my way. He's been awesome." I said, trying to fill the gaps of silence in the conversation.

"It's the least I could do," Max replied.

The silence on his end of the line was long and drawn out. I waited for him to say something, anything while pushing away the temptation to open myself to his emotions.

He hissed out a long sigh. "I would really like to see you and talk to you face to face, but I'm leaving in the morning for another assignment. I don't know how long I'll be gone."

The underlying question he'd left unsaid amounted to "will you be there when I get back?" I avoided the answer, I'd been dreaming of sun, warmth, and the beach lately.

"Take care of yourself, Max, these assignments can be hell."

He gave me a half-hearted chuckle. "Tell me about it," A couple of heartbeats later. "Take care of yourself, too. I'll be in touch."

I stared at the phone for a moment, just hearing his voice ignited a fire deep in my soul.

By the end of week three, Chase was back to his work routine and I'd graduated to light kickboxing. The Doc insisted on sticking around to keep an eye on my progress, making me wonder if he was following Max's orders.

At week four I was out hiking, riding Lightning again, and of course, playing with the cute kittens Pumpkin had given birth to. I'd still get achy sometimes, and my scars would throb, but since the blood tests continued to come back clean I brushed it aside.

Feeling almost like my normal self again I decided to see if my new abilities would work in the real world.

I contacted Bear and asked how things were going with the remodel. He invited me down for lunch and a walk through, I agreed, as long as I could bring Chase and Killer. We made plans for the next day.

I inhaled a deep breath. We'd arrived at the bar before the lunch rush and sat in my truck, in the parking lot.

"Are you sure you're ready to do this?" Chase asked for the tenth time.

"I have to do it sometime. I don't want to be a hermit for the rest of my life."

"Okay, let's get this over with."

"Have a little more confidence in me would you."

"It's been a hard winter and I'm still a tad bit on edge. I wish Max was here to help with all of this."

"This wouldn't have happened if it wasn't for Max and the people he works for."

"You can't hold a grudge forever Montana."

"I don't hold grudges, Chase. I just don't forget."

"Remind me not to get on your bad side. For the record, I still think you two would make a perfect couple."

I stepped out of the truck, ignoring his last comment. The end of January was upon us, cold seeped through my bones, but, at least, the snow storms had leveled out to

238

moderate, instead of heavy. A fire blazed and a fresh pot of coffee brewed in the restaurant.

"Anyone here?" I asked, warming my hands by the fire. I became chilly way to easy these days.

Chase retrieved some coffee for us and handed me a cup. "They must be next door."

We wandered back out into the cold with Killer and entered the next building. I stopped short. My breath almost froze into icicles inside the building.

"Hello?"

"Back here," Tree replied.

We followed Tree's voice. He stood in the back room, with a scowl on his face, and close to three feet of snow covering the floor in front of him. I looked up at the blue sky above us.

"Pops out getting the shovels and our roofing guy will be here soon, along with the plumber." Tree exclaimed, utterly disgusted. "We've been on the roofs throughout the winter, shoveling snow, and the one day Pop was sick and I had to tend the restaurant by myself, this happens." He mumbled a few words under his breath I couldn't hear, but I had an idea of what they were.

I glanced at the mess and laughed. Tree glared at me.

"It's only a small setback. Look at it this way, you were planning on taking down the roof in this area anyway, and putting up something more efficient for your greenhouse." I grinned. "You're already halfway there."

"I need to warm up." Tree growled, not seeing any humor in the situation.

We followed him back to the restaurant and sat at a table in front of the fire.

239

"I wish Rose was here, she would be a big help right now," Bear said. walking up behind us with a cup of java.

"Are you going to close for the day?"

"Nah, I'll put our earliest customer to work for an hour or two."

"I'll stay and help," Chase said, glancing at me to make sure I didn't need anything.

I smiled at him. "Is there anything I can do?"

"Naw, just a small setback, we'll get it taken care of. We may not be able to feed you today, though."

Killer whined at the comment.

"Don't worry boy, I'll make sure to send you home with something." He scratched Killers head, making him grin.

"Any idea on when Rose is coming back?" I asked.

"No, her kids won't put her on a plane until it's done snowing up here. I think if they had a choice they wouldn't let her come back at all." Bear smiled. "I'm tempted to go out there and retrieve her myself. She's tough, she can handle this."

I grinned, "Good luck with that; her kids think she's a porcelain doll. Have you spoken to Alexis?"

"Yep, her products are going to do great in our shop. I've already talked to some of the ladies around here; they can't wait."

"That's wonderful news. She gave me one of her products and I love it."

Chase got up to get us some more coffee, while we sat in silence, watching the flames crackle in the fireplace. There really wasn't much to discuss, Bear, Tree, and Alexis seemed to have everything under control. I was doing fairly

240

well keeping their energy blocked, at least, everyone's but Trees. He was suffering major anxiety attacks because of the roof caving in.

After more coffee, and some small talk, it was time to hit the road back home. Bear gave Killer a huge bone to gnaw on. I let Tree know if they needed any help with the roof to call. I left with the feeling I'd accomplished a great deal today, one more month of practice and rehab should be more than enough time to get me back on my game.

Chapter Twenty-Five

When I arrived home I was surprised to find the doc gone. I smirked. He never did tell me his real name. Whether he went out to run an errand or headed home was anyone's guess, but at least, for now, I had the house to myself. I threw my keys on the counter and ran upstairs. For some reason, I was in the mood to check on all of my business dealings. I needed to get on the computer before the mood left. I looked everything over, my net worth continued to grow at a nice pace.

I finished up and took Killer out onto the deck with me for some sunshine.

I sat on the deck relaxing when my phone buzzed. I checked the caller ID, Max. I deliberated on answering, by the time I'd made up my mind he'd hung up.

Oh well, maybe next time.

I held onto my phone, realizing that I actually kept it fully charged and with me at all times now. Frowning, I lit a smoke and turned it off. That was one habit I didn't want to start.

For The next two weeks, my life was routine. Wake up, stretch, meditate, work out, ride Lightning, and check on Pumpkin and the kittens.

The vet managed to get through the snow couple times to make sure Pumpkin and her litter were fine. He always laughed at us; said they were healthy, and asked if we'd stop calling him at every small sneeze. What he didn't understand was if something happened to kitties, Rose would kill us.

Doc never returned, Max didn't call me back, or if he had, he never left a message. The days were getting slightly warmer and it hadn't snowed since before I meet with Bear and Tree for lunch. I spent the extra time cleaning my house, which took me two days because I conquered my desk. With my life back in order, I didn't have much left to do.

I found myself checking my phone for messages every day and twiddling my thumbs. I hadn't seen much of Chase. He'd decided that, since I was doing great, he'd get caught up on work. He drifted back and forth from Rose's to Max's, inviting me to join him several times. I declined. I was ready for my vacation to be over.

I needed to decide where my next destination would be, and I needed to figure out if I'd be able to go back to work now that my sensing ability had been compromised.

On a very long, extremely boring day, I decided to let the universe pick my next destination for me. I bought a dartboard off the Internet and a map of the world.

While I waited for my goodies, I wondered again when Rose would be back. She'd been trying hard to convince her kids she needed to come home, to no avail. I didn't want to leave without her here to keep an eye on everything. Chase was too busy to do it, and ended up gone for days at a time, taking care of Max's house and whatever else he took care of.

What did he do for Max? I sighed.

"We have to get out of here, Killer," I mumbled as I pet him. "You look as bored as I am."

My map and dartboard arrived in the mail almost a week later. I quickly tore open the box and ran to my office upstairs. I hung the dart board on the wall and pinned the map to it. Grabbing the darts, I took a few steps back and threw one, then another, and another, until I didn't have any left. I examined the dartboard reviewing the places I'd hit and cringed. I didn't want to travel to any of those places.

I needed warm, beach, and sun. I stepped back and threw the darts again, not hitting one appealing place. Maybe I wouldn't leave it up to the universe. I did this for the next few hours by throwing all of the darts at once, one at a time, two at a time, and three at a time. Still nowhere I wanted to go.

The next morning I grabbed the darts and chucked them at the dartboard. Without looking I went downstairs for coffee then hit the shower. I'd just gotten dressed and turned on my phone when it rang. I picked it up, walking to the dartboard while answering.

"Hey Rose, how are you?"

"I'll be better in two days," she whispered.

"Does that mean you're coming back?"

"Yes and I can't wait. Finally! Bear's going to pick me up at the airport. What are your plans?"

I grinned. "It looks like I'm going to have to leave for a while. I'm happy you'll be back to take care of things."

"I thought Chase was doing that."

"He is, but since Max left he's been working double time. How did you do it, Rose?"

"Oh, I've been a bitter old lady this last month, bitched about everything, and have driven my kids to almost moving out of their own house."

Laughter rang in her voice.

"They decided they would send me back to drive you crazy for a while."

"It sounds like they finally came to their senses," I said with a chuckle.

"Yes, they did. I would ask you where you're going but you're never in one place for very long so it probably doesn't matter. I can't keep up anyway. How's Pumpkin?"

"Becoming a bitter old lady. She can barely move around. The kittens are constantly hungry. But don't worry we've had the vet out a few times. It's a waiting game now, and you're the perfect person to take care of her. I'll make sure she knows you are coming home to save her from her little mongrels."

Rose giggled with excitement, "I can't wait to see her. And I can't wait to meet the new babies."

"You'd better be careful Rose. Bear might start feeling left out."

"Oh, I can't wait to see Bear, either." Silence.

"What's up Rose? Is there a problem between you two?"

"No, no, but I might as well tell you now since I won't be seeing you."

I waited for a beat.

"Bear's asked me to work with him full time, and I

said yes. That won't be a problem will it?"

I laughed as I pulled the darts out of the board. I was actually expecting her to say they were getting married.

"It's not a problem. Will you still be able to take care of my garden or should I hire someone?"

"No, don't hire anyone. I love working in that room."

"Good, I miss you, Rose."

"I miss you too. Call me when you get to wherever, or better yet I'll call you when I get home."

"Talk to you later, Rose."

"And it's about time," she said before hanging up.

I spent the rest of the day packing and making double sure I had everything in order. I gave Lightning a kiss goodbye and checked on Pumpkin a couple of times. I searched around for Chase, but couldn't find him anywhere, so I headed back to my house to write him a note.

Chase,
I had to leave unexpectedly. You're more than welcome to stay in the cabin anytime you need. Rose will be back in a couple of days. Take care.
Love Montana

Authors Bio

Lynn Thompson lives in a small town in New Mexico with her husband and son. She has a degree in graphic arts and web design. In her spare time she loves to read and write. Blake is her first novel.

Sterling, the second novel staring Montana Dayton, coming out in 2012.

If you have enjoyed reading Blake please be kind and leave a review.
Lynn appreciates the feedback.

For more on Lynn Thompson visit:

Facebook
www.facebook.com/BlakeAMontanaDaytonNovel
Twitter @lynnthompson8
Website www.lynnthompsonbooks.com
Goodreads
http://www.goodreads.com/author/show/5625793.Lynn_Thompson